1

My Alien Connection 3

The Prophecy Twins

by

Vernon Gillen

All of Vernon's novels and books are available at Amazon.com

ISBN - #

978-1794088009

To The Writer

If you like to tell stories then start writing them down. You will get better over time. The hardest part in writing a novel is starting it. In writing all of my novels I have to go back to the first chapter and rewrite at least part of it. I start with an idea but, as I write I come up with more ideas that do not go along with the first chapter. That is what is so great about computers. You can always go back and change something.

One more thing. Every writer has someone that thinks what you are writing is not worthy of being published. DO NOT listen to them. Put your ideas on your computer and then publish it. My first novel was a story that I just kept writing. I ended up with a 414 page novel that I actually still have not published; yet. It is coming soon.

The main thing to remember is this. If you have a story and like to write then write. Just do it and you might be surprised at what you end up with. But you will never know if you do not do it.

Vernon Gillen

From the Author

If you have read any of my novels you will see that all of my main characters are Christians or become Christians during the novel. This is because I am a Christian although some of my friends may say that I do not talk like one. All through all of my novels the main character prays asking God for help.

In any of my novels where I introduce aliens from other planets I make it a point to mention that even they worship the same God and Jesus that we Christians on Earth do although they call them by different names.

I believe that God created all life on Earth and therefore must have also created any on other planets. How could God have created the planets and not the life on them? I do not believe that all life on Earth came from a mixture of amino acids that stuck together and then walked out on land and became man. That's just stupid.

So what I am trying to say is that I put into my novels things that I believe. Unfortunately: this also means politics. Boy here's a can of worms here.

I am not a Republican but I am not a Liberal Communist either. I am a Conservative that votes straight Republican. In all of my novels I call all Liberals, and even just Democrats Communist. This is why.

Make a list of what the Communist want in this country in order to destroy this country. Now make a list of what the Liberals and Democrats want in order to "save" this country. Both lists are the same starting with taking my guns. Therefore; all Liberals and even just Democrats are Communist. If you do not like my saying that then it is simple. Don't buy my novels.

I use things that I have seen, learned, and experienced during my life in my novels. Any good write will do this. Some really gory things I probably have not experienced. Those things come from my overworked and warped imagination. When you read something really gory in one of my novels just

6

remember that I was probably thinking at the time that I wrote it of what I would like to do to a Liberal Communist. They are the enemies of this nation bent on destroying this nation. They are my enemy; your enemy, and the enemy of any patriotic American.

I was not raised in the country but my father and grandpa did take me hunting and fishing a great deal. Now at age sixty-four as I write this I do live in the country. I hunt and fish and eat what I kill of catch. I actually dated a women one time (and only one time) that believed that hamburger meat grew on a tree like moss. Just how stupid could she get. How does meat grow on a plant? Think about it. Needless to say but I'll say it anyway. She was a city girl.

I have been asked why I have cursing in my novels if I am a Christian. This is because not everyone is a Christian and I am trying to make my novel as realistic as possible. Many readers picture themselves in the novel that they are reading. In their reality they are experiencing what they are reading. For this reason some of the characters in my novels use foul language.

Well this is me in a nutshell. I hope you enjoy my novels. If you do then look at the end of this novel where you will find my e-mail address and web site. Let me know what you think about this novel. Feel free to give me any ideas or thought you might have. Thank you for buying this novel.

Contents

Chapter 1

Troubled Child

The people of Stylus had not seen any hint of Zim warships or Superships for many years. The Stylus military had become relaxed and soft. And yet unknown to the Stylus the Zim had been building Superships on many planets on the other side of the galaxy. All hell was about to be unleashed on Stylus.

The Prophecy Twins were now seventeen year old. The struggled between their training and problems that all teenagers had. They wanted to be free to do as they wished but their training kicked in and self-discipline kept them above other teens. Every move their bodies made had a reason and purpose. They had been raised having no contact with other teens except for their cousins.

Revis and Lesst had a fifteen year old son named Nash. Rommin and Tesh also got married and had a fourteen year old son named Rome. Rome and Nash were wild young men but their parents kept them in check and out of trouble.

Being raised away from other children Johm and Meshet kept to themselves. Being twins might have had something to do with it but they both knew what the other was thinking. Then Johm made some friends in the city and started spending time with them.

"You two okay?" Bubba asked Johm and Meshet who were sitting in the kitchen of their home. Meshet was much like her sister Lesst. Seeing her father she jumped up an hugged him. "What are you two up to?"

"We were just wondering what our purpose is in relation to the prophecy." Johm said. "We have not heard from the Zim since we were tiny babies and somehow we are suppose to be the saviors of the Stylus people."

9

"You're the savior of the Stylus people Dad." Meshet said.

"I understand how you feel but your mom … like millions of Stylus still think that you both are the prophesied twins." Bubba told his two kids. "Actually … I believe it too."

"But it doesn't make since Dad." Meshet calmly said.

"Maybe it will later." Bubba added. "Be patient. I know there are more Zim out there but I just don't know where they are or what they are up to."

"But it's been almost fifteen years." Meshet mentioned. "What can they do in that time?"

"Grow in numbers and build more Superships." Bubba advised.

Bubba got another mug of coffee and walked out on the porch. Sitting down at the table he looked over the city in front of him and then the lake to the right of the city. Families were enjoying themselves on the lake beach and in their boats on the lake. Johm got himself a mug of coffee and joined his father.

I heard the other day that the Russian president you fought had a son." Johm said. "His son has taken over the country."

"After I brought the Kremlin down on Petrov someone else would take over." Bubba advised. "How did his son get control?"

"Our teacher didn't say." Johm answered. "Maybe we just don't know."

"The hybrid spies on Earth are still sending information to us." Bubba informed his son. "I'll see if one of them knows anything.

When the teacher walked up on the porch Johm went back inside. He and Meshet did their schooling at home.

"Good morning Miss Daimy." Bubba said.

"And good morning to you to Mister Prime Minister." Daimy said. She looked over the city and lake. "It is so beautiful up here."

"Yes it is." Bubba replied. God … I mean Muchee has really blessed me."

"Meshet told me what happened to your home on Earth …

how the government destroyed it." Daimy advised.

"And ... Muchee ... has paid me back ten times what they took from just as it is written in his word.

The Zim and Stylus worshiped the same god that Christians on Earth did. And like on Earth he sent his son to die for their sins. Muchee is just the name the Stylus call their Jesus.

Daimy went into the home smiling but Becka came out to be with her husband. Sitting at the table with a mug of hot cocoa she looked over the city and lake.

"I love it so much out here." Becka said with a big smile. "It reminds me of our home on Earth except that it is much prettier here."

"I love it here too." Bubba agreed.

"Meshet was talking to me earlier about her brother." Becka informed her husband.

"Something wrong?"

"She is concerned about him." Becka continued. "She said that he has been getting rebellious the past few months."

"I haven't seen it. He's always nice around me and does what I tell him to do."

"Remember last month when he hit Revis' and Lesst's son Nash?"

"I forgot about that." Bubba said as he looked down. "But he only slapped Nash."

"Assault is still assault." Becka said. "You should know that ... Prime Minister. Aren't you the keeper of the law?"

"Oh that was a low blow Babe." Bubba informed his wife.

"The only reason Johm did not go to jail was because he is your son. And you never did talk to him about it."

Bubba knew that she was right. He also knew that Johm was nothing like his two brothers Rommin and Coman. His two sisters Lesst and Meshet were perfect ladies. Becka saw to that. Suddenly he felt as if he was a failure as a father. He felt that he failed his son Johm by not being stricter. Johm's attitude must be his fault.

"I'll talk to him when he break for lunch." He informed

11

his wife.

"Thank you Baby." Becka said. "Being one of the Prophecy Twins he should be above everyone else."

"I know Babe."

Becka stood and gave her husband a kiss on the forehead. Then she went back in the house. Bubba sighed heavily as he looked over the sites below. He had conquered the Zim in many battles but he could not control a seventeen year old boy. Where did he go wrong? He never had problems with Rommin and Coman or his two girls Lesst and Meshet.

With his coffee mug empty Bubba got up and walked in the house. As he passed Johm he leaned over and whispered in his son's ear. ""I need to talk to you when you break for lunch."

"Yes Dad." There was no problem there so Bubba got his coffee and went back out on the porch. About two hours later Johm and Meshet broke for lunch. Johm got himself a glass of ice tea and went out on the porch finding his father asleep in his chair.

"Dad." Johm said as he gently shook his father's shoulder.

"What." Bubba said as he woke up from his nap. Bubba was no longer a young man at the age of eighty-three. Becka was one hundred thirteen and still looked like she was about thirty.

"You said you wanted to talk to me." Johm reminded his father.

"Yes." Bubba said as he sat up in his chair. "I need to talk to you about something."

Bubba started talking to his son about his slapping his younger and smaller cousin. He did not look at Johm as he talked. If he had he would have seen the anger building up in his son's eyes. Finally Johm had enough and quickly stood.

"I'm tired of you and others telling me what to do." he yelled loud enough that everyone in the house came outside. "I'm one of the Prophecy Twins. You can't tell me what to do." Then he raise his hand and was about to strike his father when Meshet jumped at him and grabbed his arm.

"Don't even think about it." Meshet yelled at her brother. "I can take you down anytime you want and you know it."

Without any warning Johm calmed down. "I'm sorry father." he said as he started to cry. Then he quickly went into the house and his bedroom shutting the door behind him.

"Where did that come from?" Becka asked Bubba.

"I don't know." he said as Meshet hugged him. "Did you notice something about his crying?"

"No Dad." Meshet said. "What about it?"

"He cried a good half minutes before leaving and yet there were no tears."

"How do you know he didn't cry?" Meshet asked.

"He leaned over the table as he cried and yet it is dry." Bubba mentioned. "Also he looked up before leaving and I could see that his eyes were dry as well."

"Oh he is a good actor." Meshet said. "I've seen him act sick ... or whatever ... many times to get out of some training he did not want to go to. Then later he would laugh about it when we were alone."

"Why have you not told me about this earlier?"

"Didn't know you wanted to know." Meshet replied. "I'm sorry Dad."

"Oh it's okay Baby Doll." Bubba assured her. "Now his instructors need to know."

"Oh they all know but he is such a good actor that they do not know if he is really sick or not." Meshet informed her father. "They did not want one of the Prophecy Twins not seeing the medical team just in case he was sick."

"Johm does not need to know that we had this talk." Bubba insisted.

"Yes Sir." Meshet agreed. So did everyone else there.

Johm came out of his bedroom when class began again. No one let him know that his father was watching him now. Johm acted normal the rest of the day but went out that night. He had friends and a girlfriend that he spent much of his time with.

What Johm did not know was that although he had

security with him at all times two of his hybrid friends were actually Zim spies. They were both his age and were working on convincing him to join the Stylus resistance. Many of the young Stylus and hybrids were starting to join this new underground group.

Meshet stayed at home and away from others. She saw her being one of the Prophecy Twins as a big responsibility. She was very disappointed in Johm.

Later Bubba went to bed early. As he walked by Meshet's bedroom he heard her crying. Pushing her open door farther open he stepped in her room.

"You okay Meshet?" a concerned father asked.

Instantly Meshet started wiping the tears from her face as if she was hiding them. "I'm okay Dad."

"You want to try that lie again?" Bubba asked.

"We're loosing Johm." Meshet said as she cried more. Then she went on to tell her father more about Johm.

"I'll take care of this." Bubba assured his daughter. "And this conversation never took place either."

"Yes Sir." Meshet said through her sniffles.

The next morning Bubba sat at his desk. The first thing that he did was call into his office the security that fallowed Johm. An hour later four of the security walked into his office.

"You're the ones that are watching over my son Johm when he goes out at night?"

Three of the security spoke English so Bubba pointed at one of them and ordered him to make sure the forth one knew what was being said.

"My son goes out almost every night and hangs out with a few friends and his girlfriend." Bubba said. "Do any of you know these friends of his?"

One of the security quickly spoke up. "Two ... maybe three of them are hard core Sir."

"What do you mean hard core?"

"They are in trouble all of the time." another one of the security said. "Your son is hanging around some of the young that ... I think are members of the resistance movement."

14

Bubba dismissed the security after reminding them that Johm did not need to know about the meeting. They all agreed. As the security left Bubba's office he broke out some paper and started writing. He wrote a law to be cleared with the King outlawing gangs and other organizations that plotted against the government or committed crimes. Then he took it to Yunnan for him to look over.

Bubba told Yunnan why he wrote it and also mentioned that the resistance group was quickly growing. "If we do not do something fast we will have problems later ... bad problems."

That night soldiers went out into the city and grabbed anyone that they felt was part of the resistance group. Judge Jester would take care of most of those brought in. It would be his job to learn if they are apart of the resistance and then put them in prison if they were.

One special team was sent to where Johm hung out. Without any warning the team grabbed Johm's friends and brought them to the palace jail. To make it look good Johm was also grabbed and thrown in the jail with his friends. Security informed Bubba that his son had been arrested and was in the palace jail. He would let his son stew overnight in the packed cell. Bubba hoped that his son spending the night in jail might put a dent in his thinking that he was above the law.

The next morning Bubba went into the courtroom and had the prisoners brought to him. Seeing his son standing before him he tried to look puzzled.

"Johm?" Bubba asked. "Why are you with this ... trash?"

Instantly the six young trouble makers started yelling but an electric rod convinced them to shut up. Johm knew he was in enough trouble and was not yelling.

"You want to answer me Johm?" Bubba asked.

Johm said nothing but slowly stepped up to his father's desk. The judge's desk which Bubba sat behind was up on a platform so Johm had to look up at his father.   "Yes Sir." Johm said as he looked down.

For about a minute Bubba just stared at Johm saying nothing. Then he said; "Go home Johm. You really need to be

15

there when I get home."

"Yes Sir. Johm said as he turned and left for home.

When Johm left the courtroom Bubba spoke to the others. "Because I did not come down on my son I will not come down on any of you. Three of you have criminal records and do not need to be around my son." Bubba looked at the two women. "Which one of you is dating my son?"

One hybrid woman stepped up. "I am … Prime Minister."

"You have a criminal record. You hit a child hurting her badly. Is this true?"

"Yes Sir." the girl confessed.

"Well at least you are honest." Bubba said. "But you will not be seeing Johm again. Do you understand?"

"Yes Sir." she said again.

Bubba dismissed the others and sent them home with a warning. "Stay away from my son."

Bubba had no idea that two of the young adults that stood in front of him were Zim spies including the woman with the criminal record. She was Johm's girlfriend.

That evening after a long day of work as Prime Minister Bubba went to Yunnan's office to talk with him. He told Yunnan what he had done and why. Yunnan shook his head from side to side. "Did I do something wrong Sir?" Bubba asked.

"Oh no." Yunnan let him know. "I just hate seeing this happen with one of the Prophecy Twins."

Neither men could think of anything else to do other than what Bubba had already done. Then Bubba suggested talking to all of Johm's instructors. Yunnan agreed. This was not just a father intervening a bothered child. Johm was one of the Prophecy Twins and he needed to start acting like it.

Bubba went home expecting Johm to be gone against his wishes. However; Johm was home studying his Stylus history books. When the family ate the evening meal Johm was acting like the old Johm. He looked happy and even smiled a few times. But Bubba did not think his son was being honest. *Could he just be acting again*? Bubba had no way of knowing until he looked over at Meshet.

Meshet looked at her father. Making eye contact with her father she slowly shook her head from side to side. Bubba then was sure that Johm was acting again. Johm and Meshet could always know what the other was thinking. As she looked away from her father she looked at Johm who was staring at her. He knew what she was shaking her head for.

After dinner Johm walked up to Meshet and said; "I never thought that you would turn against me."

"I haven't turned against you." Meshet got into her brother's face. "You have turned against all of us. You have turned against the prophecy of us being the saviors of our people."

"Our people?" Johm asked. "That prophecy is for the Stylus not us hybrids."

"We are Stylus citizens now and you know it." Meshet told her brother. "The prophecy is for us as well."

Johm said nothing else and walked into his room. For a while Meshet just stood there looking at Johm's closed bedroom door. She could read his thoughts and finally realized that she had already lost her brother. His heart was full of hate but she could not see who he hated. That was buried deep in his heart where she could not see.

The next day Bubba went to his office and found a security officer waiting for him. He told Bubba that Yunnan wanted to see him as quickly as possible. When he walked into Yunnan's office the King stood and smiled.

"There you are my friend." Yunnan said.

"Oh my." Bubba said. "When you call me your friend that usually means that you want something of me."

"I do but sit down and let's talk a minute." Yunnan advised.

"I like what you wrote up about gangs and the resistance movement." Yunnan said. "All of these are young people that have no respect for our planet. A few are older mental midgets that should know better. Our people used to be law abiding Stylus citizens but for some reason these young people have started acting more like Zim than Stylus."

"I know Sir." Bubba agreed. "This happened in my country on Earth as well. Just like on Earth the young people will push the limits of the law and if nothing is done they will start rioting and killing your police and soldiers. We must stop it now."

"I agree." Yunnan said. "That's why I have passed your ideas into law. It is now a high crime to be a member of a group or gang that is a movement against the government."

"In the papers I gave you this would be a crime if the members start rioting and causing damage to the city or state of Stylus."

"That is right." Yunnan agreed. "A member of one of these groups or gangs would not be a criminal unless the members start rioting and destroying property or hurting citizens. Then that group or gang would be an outlaw group or gang and it's members criminals.

"Is this want you want to talk to me about?" Bubba inquired.

"Not really." Yunnan said. "As you know all citizens have the right to carry firearms in the public." Yunnan said. "Now that we are no longer at war with the Zim should we stop that?"

"If you do that then crime will go up." Bubba advised.

"There is a growing group of citizens that want all firearms outlawed." Yunnan advised his Prime Minister.

"You will not live forever and when you are replaced that person could try to become a dictator." Bubba explained. "That dictator could make it really bad for the citizens of Stylus."

"I know." Yunnan said. "You have talked to me about this before and I see what you mean. Yushera and I have been trying to have a son but she is now barren and cannot have any children. That means that by law you would step up to be King."

"I still say that the citizens should keep the right to carry firearms in public." Bubba insisted. "Private ownership of firearms and the ability to protect your home and yourself will keep anyone from trying to become a dictator. Carrying a firearm allows a citizen to protect themselves and crimes against another citizen are growing on Stylus."

Yunnan thought for a moment and then agreed with Bubba. A citizen still has the right to carry a firearm in public and at their homes.

For a while Johm stayed at home instead of going out on the town with his friends. It seemed that he finally embraced his calling as one of the Prophecy Twins. If he was acting again then he was good at it and was even fooling his sister.

Chapter 2

Tough Love

For two weeks Johm stayed at home studying. His evenings were now spend reading and studying things he might need as one of the Prophecy Twins. But finally the wild side of him started to come out again. One night he went out to meet his friends and this time he left home without any security to watch over him.

"Hello everyone." Johm said as he walked up to his friends.

"Well well." the group leader and Zim spy, Stogy said. "The dead has come back to us."

Stogy was one of the Zim spies and very happy to see Johm again. Now he can get back to convincing Johm to joining the resistance. But now he had a different goal; a different mission. He had orders to convince Johm to join the Zims.

"So where is your security?" Johm's girlfriend, Obi asked.

"I got tired of having them around so I left without them." Johm said.

Stogy and Obi looked at each other and smiled. This may be the chance that they had been looking for. A plan began to form in Stogy's mind. He whispered into Obi's ear causing her to smile again.

"Ha Johm." Obi said. "Let's all go to the shipyard."

"Why?" Johm asked.

"Your dad likes coffee doesn't he?" Stogy asked.

"He loves it."

"Well I know where there is a lot of it in a few containers." Stogy informed Johm. "We can take some of it and give it to your father. That might make him happy enough to lay off of us for a while."

"I don't know Stogy." Johm said shaking his head from

side to side. "If I get caught doing that then I would be in a lot more trouble."

"But the containers are in a dark area and the police still think that all Stylus are basically honest." Stogy mentioned. "They don't think anyone will take any of it."

An hour later Johm and his friends found themselves at the shipyard. Stogy pointed at the containers that held the coffee in them. The group took their time sneaking up to the corner of a building. But as they left that building they crossed an open area that had lights. A cargo ship taking off into the air reported seeing the kids. The Shipyard Security was called.

Stogy broke the seal on the container door and opened it. Then he and Johm stepped inside finding the container almost full of one hundred pound bags of coffee. Suddenly a voice outside ordered them all to stop. As the five outside started to run the security opened fire hitting two of them. The two women and one young man got away. One of the men that got shot died there. The other one was badly wounded.

Shipyard Security stood outside the container and ordered anyone inside to come out. Stogy and Johm slowly walked out with their hands in the air.

"Are we in trouble?" Stogy asked the security hoping for a laugh.

Saying nothing to them the security handcuffed Stogy and Johm. Then they were taken to the city jail. The wounded man was taken to the hospital where he also died.

The next morning Bubba got up and looked into Johm's bedroom. His bed was still made showing that he went out that night and had still not come home. Sitting down at the kitchen table Becka brought him a mug of coffee.

"Johm went out last night again and still has not come home." Bubba told his wife.

Becka left the sausage cooking and ran to Johm's bedroom. Seeing the made bed she walked back into the kitchen and took the sausage out of the frying pan. Setting the plate of sausage on the table she sat down. At that time Meshet walked into the kitchen and sat at the table.

"Where do you think he is?" Becka asked Bubba.

"Where who is?" Meshet asked.

"Your brother went out again last night and still has not come home." Becka said.

"That's what I felt last night." Meshet said. "He's in trouble."

"Where is he Meshet?" Bubba asked his daughter.

Meshet closed her eyes and concentrated. "He's in jail ... again."

Bubba took in a deep breath and let it out. "I'll do something but if he committed a crime ... my hands will be tied."

Becka put on hand on her husband's hand. "Be easy on him Baby."

"That's the problem." Bubba said as he stood. "I have been easy on him. Now it's time for some tough love."

Bubba got dressed and walked down the hill to the palace and then into his office. He called the city jail and asked about Johm.

"He was here Sir." the head jailer said. "When we realized who he was we had him transferred to the palace jail for you."

"Thank you but I may be transferring him back to you."

"Just let me know what you want done Prime Minister."

"Thanks again." Bubba said as he stood and walked into Yunnan's office.

"There you are." Yunnan said. "I didn't hear you walk in."

Bubba sat down and told Yunnan what had happened.

"Wow!" Yunnan said. "That puts the whole gang on the list of outlawed gangs now. This could put them on the list for execution."

"They were stopped before they took anything." Bubba informed the King.

"At least that will keep them off of the execution list but he still could be given life in prison."

"Yes Sir. I know." a very depressed Prime Minister said. I am his father but I am the people's Prime Minister first."

"No." Yunnan insisted. "You're a father having problems

with his son first. Then you are my Prime Minister."

"I let him get away with slapping his cousin." Bubba said. "I let him get away when we had that gang members round-up. Sooner or later I have to put my foot down."

"I feel for you but I also know that you're right." Yunnan said. "I'll stand behind you in whatever you do."

"Thank you Sir." Bubba said and then stood to leave. "I'll keep you informed as to what I do."

"Sounds good my friend." Yunnan said.

Bubba left Yunnan's office and went into his own office. He contacted the city jail and had Stogy brought to the palace jail. An hour later Stogy and Johm stood before the Prime Minister in the palace court. Trying to show no partiality he judged the two.

"You two have been charged with breaking into a container at the shipyard and attempting to steel coffee. How do you plea?"

"We were trying to get the coffee for you Mister Prime Minister." Stogy admitted.

"So your plea is guilty?" Bubba asked.

"No Sir." Stogy said thinking about what he had said.

"And you ... Johm." Bubba said looking right into his eyes. "How do you plea?"

"I didn't do anything wrong." Johm smarted off.

"So trespassing and breaking into a container to steal what was inside is legal now?"

"No no." Johm quickly said. "I didn't mean that."

"Well ... were your actions last night legal or illegal?" Bubba asked his son.

Johm was quiet knowing that no matter how he answered the question he would still be in trouble.

"I find both of you guilty of trespassing and breaking into a container with the intent to steal the contents of that container. I will not charge you with the deaths of two of your friends which you both are responsible for. I sentence you both to sixty days of hard labor at the rock quarry."

"But Dad ..." Johm yelled as security took the two away.

When the two were gone Bubba started crying.

"Am I a bad father Lord? I could have ... and should have given them both at least a year but because Johm was one of the two I didn't do it. I have tried to be nice but Johm just used that against me. Please help me Father. Please guide me in this."

Bubba thought for a moment and realized that he did the right thing. If the sixty days does not curve his son's attitude then next time he would give his son a longer sentence.

Later that evening Bubba took a transport up the hill to his home. Walking up the hill was becoming quite a chore with his age creeping up on him. Walking downhill in the mornings was no problem; yet.

Once Bubba got into the home and got himself a glass of ice tea he sat down in his chair in the den. Sitting on the other side of a small table between the two chairs was Becka reading her novel.

"What did you do with Johm?" Becka asked.

"I gave him and his friend sixty days at the rock quarry."

"You want?" Becka was shocked.

"Two of his friends were killed because of their actions." Bubba told his wife. "They trespassed on the shipyard property and broke into a container of coffee. Stogy even admitted that they were stealing the coffee for me ... or at least that was his story. I could have given them both one year but didn't."

"But two months of hard labor." Becka argued.

"I've been nice to many times and it is not working." Bubba defended his actions. "Now it is time for some tough love."

"And you might have chased your son away for good."

"Then let that be his decision."

Upstairs Meshet stood at the door of her bedroom listening to what was being said. She slowly closed her door and lay on her bed crying. She thought about what her father said and she agreed that it was time for tough love. She fell asleep still crying.

* * * * *

Stogy and Johm were taken to the city jail where they spent the night. The next morning they were transferred to the rock quarry. Once inside the fence they were taken to a building where they were booked and given their pink jumpsuits. Then they were taken to the barracks where they would spend the next two months. They would start their sentence the next morning.

For the first time in his life Johm would be facing other men without the protection of security watching over him. For the next two months he would have to handle all of his problems himself.

That evening the prisoners came into the barracks from their day's work breaking up large rocks with sledge hammers. "Fresh meat." one of them yelled.

"I think we should have taken our shower before they came in." Johm told Stogy.

"You just need to let them know that you're not scared of them." Stogy informed his young friend. "Here's what you need to do."

Stogy stood and walked up to the biggest prisoner in the barracks. Suddenly Stogy swung his fist hitting the big man in the face. Stogy knew that he was in trouble when the big man looked back at him and smiled. The big man spent the next two minutes beating Stogy badly. When he stopped he looked at Johm and asked if he wanted some as well. Johm threw up his hands and said; "No."

In order to keep Johm safe he was booked in as a hybrid from the other side of the planet. No one needed to know who he really was. If any of the prisoners knew that he was the son of the Prime Minister his life would be in danger. However he was still booked in under the name Johm.

The prisoners had one hour to get their shower. Then they were taken to the lunchroom where they got their food and then sat down to eat. A man across the table from Johm reached across the table and grabbed Johm's bread.

"Were you born retarded or is it something that you have to work at every day?" Johm asked the man.

"Consider it payment." the man said." I didn't kick your ass when you got here."

Johm reached across the table and took his bread back. "Consider that payment that I didn't kick your ass when I get here."

The man look mad at first and then smiled. "I like this guy." he said as he reached across the table to take the bread back.

Instantly Johm stabbed the man's hand with his fork. The man yelled out in pain. After pulling the fork out of his hand the man leaped across he table at Johm. Using his training he grabbed the man's head and forced his face into the table braking the man's nose. However this just made matters worse.

The man crawled over the table and on top of Johm. Johm quickly turned throwing the man to the floor. A quick kick left the man's jaw broken. The fight was over when security came in and separated the two. Both men were taken to separate holding cells. The other man was taken to the prison hospital.

A medical team came to see to Johm's cuts and bruises so that he would not be in the prison hospital with the man he fought. That might cause the two to fight again in the hospital itself.

Stogy was also in the hospital. He had nothing to do with the man that Johm hurt but being Johm's friend he was kept separated from the other man. If the other man found out that he and Johm were friends he might attack him in the hospital.

Johm was released from solitary confinement after serving five days. Johm took advantage of it and rested. Being alone was much better than smashing rocks with a twelve pound sledge hammer. But now he was being taken back to the rock quarry where he was handed a sledge hammer and given a large rock to work on.

Armed security was heavy in the rock quarry. The quarry itself was a large hole with plenty of large hard rocks. With only one way out of this hole the sides of the quarry were about fifteen feet high. There were no fences except around the entrance to the quarry.

That evening the prisoners came in from a day of braking up rocks. As they took their showers and then ate dinner government contractors came into the quarry and set explosives. When the explosions went off the entire area shook. This gave the prisoners more rocks to break up the next day.

The next day the prisoners were taken back to the quarry to do what they did best. About an hour later Stogy was brought out to the quarry as well. Working beside Johm they were able to talk.

"If we are to survive in this place we need to stick together." Stogy advised Johm. Johm agreed.

When Stogy and Johm were released from prison they went straight to the two women that had escaped the shipyard security. The man that had escaped with the women had not been see since hat night. Stogy and Obi needed to get together and compare notes. Obi had been staying in contact with other Zim on Stylus keeping their superiors informed of what was going on. She had already informed them that Stogy and Johm would be getting out of prison that day. After hugging Obi for a while Johm said that he needed to get home.

"You want to go home after you father put you in prison for two months?" Obi asked. "Are you crazy?"

"If I don't he will probably come looking for me." Johm said. "That would cause us all problems."

"He's right." Stogy said. "He needs to play the game and get his father off of our backs." Then Stogy grabbed Johm's shoulder. "Go see your family and act like you learned your lesson. Come see us in about a month."

Johm thought for a moment. He agreed with Stogy but was also starting to see that maybe his father was right about his friends. He left his friends and girlfriend and did not look back. He walked into the palace and into his father's office.

"Good to see you're out." Bubba said as he stood. "I heard that you did well in there ... working hard and obeying the security."

"Yeah will ... I told them what they wanted to hear." Johm said not realizing that his last remark told his father that he might try that on him as well. Bubba knew that he was going to have to keep watching his son.

Johm left and went home where he found his bedroom still undisturbed. He took a shower and then a long nap.

Knowing that he had to still do something he wrote a proclamation that no one that has been in prison may associate with others that have been in prison. This should keep Johm away from Stogy and the others. Bubba took the proclamation to Yunnan. Yunnan looked it over and then signed it into law.

That night Bubba sat at the dinner table with Becka, Johm, and Meshet. Speaking to Becka he said that Yunnan had just signed into law that no one that had been in prison may associate with others that have been in prison.

"So I can't see my friends and girlfriend again." Johm said with an angry tone.

Bubba thought and then said; Your girlfriend has not been in prison." Bubba said not knowing that she was a Zim spy. "Now Stogy has been in prison so you can no longer associate with him."

"Well just take all of my friends from me then." Johm yelled and left the dinner table. Walking into his room he lay on his bed.

Not knowing that his sister fallowed him she knocked on his door. Johm quickly rolled over and saw Meshet standing there.

"Oh ... it's you." he said as she walked in.

"Johm." her voice was always so soft and soothing. "Why is it that you cannot see your calling? It is my calling too."

"Are you stupid?" Johm said making sure not to yell. That would only bring his father upstairs. "How can we be the Prophecy Twins to save the Stylus people if Dad has already done it fifteen years ago?"

28

"Sometimes I still see the Zim rising and attacking us again." If you will open your mind you will see it too. But right now your mind is clouded with hate and anger. It has blinded you."

Meshet quickly turned and walk into her room. If anyone could reach Johm it would be his sister. Johm thought about what Meshet said. He knew that she was right but also wrestled with his desire to be with his friends. He stood and walk to his sister's bedroom door.

"Dad said that I could still see Obi." he reminded her. "You want'a go with me?"

"You betcha." Meshet happily said. She was back to doing things with her brother and that made her happy. She had been missing that. Before leaving she did tell their mom. Then she ran out of the house and joined her brother.

About an hour later Bubba came home. Becka welcomed him home and then told him about Johm and Meshet going to see his girlfriend, Obi. He was concerned at first but dismissed his fears because Meshet was with him.

"What do you think about his girlfriend, Obi?" Becka asked Bubba.

"I think I only met her once but don't remember if she was in trouble or not." he said. "I'm not even sure if I have met her." He said as he looked up at his wife. "Am I getting older?"

"Not at all my love." Becka assured her husband while giving him a hug. "You're that fine bottle of wine that I had spent all my life looking for."

Bubba smiled. "I love you too Babe."

Chapter 3

Kidnapped

Johm did as Stogy instructed him to do. He played the game convincing his parents that he had come back to them and was no longer hanging around his old friends. From time to time he left to meet his girlfriend Obi but that was all. Most of those times Meshet went with him. Johm only took his sister with him so that she would tell their parents that he was back on the straight and narrow way.

One time Johm and Meshet went to see Obi and found Stogy at her apartment. Johm was not happy to see Stogy and wondered why he was there.

"You seeing my girl now?" Johm asked Stogy.

"Not at all Johm." Stogy replied. "The only way I can find out how you are doing is by asking Obi." Then he shook Johm's hand. "I need to leave because we are not suppose to be together but first … who is this pretty thing?"

"This is my sister Meshet." Johm told Stogy.

"Well hello Beautiful." Stogy said as he walked up to Meshet.

Meshet sensed something was wrong. This man was not who he pretended to be. "You touch me and I'll kill you."

Stogy threw up his hands and said; "Woe now." Stepping back he added; "You're to rough for me."

"Let's go Johm." Meshet suggested. "The stench in this place is intolerable."

"I'll come back another time." Johm told Obi. "I need to get Meshet home before she kills Stogy." Then he looked at Stogy and said; "I'm sure you're leaving my girl's apartment as well … right?"

"Oh I see what you're getting at." Stogy said. "There's nothing to worry about. "She is my sister."

Johm looked at Obi. "He's your brother?"

"We have the same mother but different fathers." she advised Johm. Of course this was not true but it made a good story and explained why Stogy would be at Obi's apartment later.

Johm gave Obi a hug and kiss and then he and Meshet left. As they walked away from Obi's apartment Meshet spoke her mind.

"I don't like that … Stogy." she informed her brother. "If you were to concentrate like you used to you would see it too."

"I'm not sure if I can do that anymore." Johm said.

When Johm and Meshet got back home they sat in the den. Meshet tried to help her brother concentrate and see what she saw in Stogy. But Johm was just playing the game with her as well as with his parents. He was not even concentrating. His thoughts were on Obi.

Meshet could sense that her brother was not really trying. She even saw his thoughts about Obi.

"You're not even going to try?" Meshet asked Johm.

"I am trying." Johm insisted.

"You're thinking about Obi."

Johm realized that his sister was actually reading his mind. He got up and walked into his bedroom. Laying on his bed he wondered just how much his sister knew. Instead of embracing the prophecy he turned against it. All through the next day he allowed this to stew in his mind. Twice the teacher had to slap the table to shake him back into the class. The second time she slapped the table he blew up and went into his room.

About an hour later Meshet finished her class for the day and the teacher left. Meshet went into Johm's room but he was not there. He had sneaked out of the house with no one seeing him. The only way down from the second floor of the home was by the stairs and she would have seen him coming down. She saw nothing. She checked his bedroom window and it was still locked from the inside. That meant that he was getting sneakier.

Meshet told her mom what had happened and that she was

going after her brother. He had to have gone to see Obi.

Meshet walked down the road without any security with her. Finally she came upon the apartment building in which Obi lived. When she got to Obi's door she could hear both Johm and Stogy talking.

"I really think you need to come with us." Stogy told Johm. "You can't hang around here anymore."

"It's the only place where you'll be safe." Obi mentioned.

"I don't think so you little whore." Meshet said as she stepped in the apartment and closed the door behind her.

Instantly Obi grabbed Meshet and started fighting her. Stogy pulled his fist back to hit Meshet but found a knife point at his throat. Johm was holding the knife.

"Back off you son of a whore." Johm said keeping the knife point at Stogy's throat.

"Damn Johm." Stogy said as he lowered his fist and backed up.

Catching Obi off balance Meshet threw her a few feet away. "Johm?" she said.

"Let's go Meshet." Johm said.

"Can't let you do that my friend." Stogy said as he stuck a syringe needle in Johm's arm. As Meshet reached out for her brother Obi quickly jabbed a needle in Meshet's leg. Within seconds both Johm and Meshet were knocked out.

Stogy called for some help to carry Johm back to the shipyard. Once there Johm was thrown lain in an empty container. The door was closed and locked. Then the container was loaded on a ship. When the cargo ship was cleared it lifted off into the sky. Then the ship left Stylus airspace.

Back at the apartment Meshet woke up the next morning all alone. Still under he effects of the drug in her body she staggered out of the apartment and fell on the ground outside. Someone saw her and called the police.

The next time Meshet woke up she was in the hospital. Sitting in a chair to her right was her mother. Her father was just walking into the room.

"Mom." Meshet said.

Becka got up and stood beside the bed. "You'll be okay." her mother said. "Where is your brother?"

Bubba walked back into the room after flagging down the police chief that was investigating what had happened.

"What happened to you and your brother?" the police chief asked Meshet.

Meshet told everyone what happened. She told them about the fight and that Obi was involved in Johm's kidnapping. Then the police chief left to start his investigation.

"This is why you do not leave without security with you." Bubba scorned his daughter. "You could have been taken too."

"The doctor said that you had been injected with enough of the drug to kill you so they wanted you dead." Becka told her daughter.

"What I don't understand is why they only kidnapped your brother and not both of you." Bubba mentioned. "Ever since you two were born the Zim have been wanting both of you. Now ... having the chance to get you both they only took Johm.

"Maybe because they already had him convinced to take the side of the Zim." Meshet suggested.

"Can you see where your brother is?" Bubba asked Meshet.

Meshet closed her eyes and concentrated. "He's in a dark place." She tried a little more but added; "That's all I can see. He is in a dark place where he is feeling around."

"That's okay Baby Doll." Bubba said. "We'll find him and Stogy and Obi will both be executed for this and for trying to kill you."

Bubba had to get back to his work at the palace while Becka and seven of the palace security stayed with Meshet. When Becka came home two of the security officers would go back with her.

Hearing Judge Jester in the palace courtroom Bubba stepped inside. Jester stopped everything. "May I help you Prime Minister?"

Bubba walked up to the judge's desk and whispered into

Jester's ear. He told Jester what had happened. Then he asked Jester to watch for any cases against the palace or the government. "Send these cases to me. And also watch for two hybrids named Stogy and Obi. They are the ones that kidnapped my son."

"You bet I will Sir." Judge Jester agreed.

Bubba left the courtroom and Jester got back to handling court problems. Bubba went to see Yunnan.

"I heard about Meshet and Johm my friend." Yunnan told Bubba as he walked into the office and sat down. "Is she okay?"

"She will be Sir." Bubba said. "I just need to stay busy."

"I understand." Yunnan said.

Bubba left Yunnan's office and went into his office. Coman looked at his father. "You going to be okay Dad?" Coman asked.

Bubba took in a deep breath and let it out. "I think so." The truth was that he had no idea where to look. He, and everyone else still thought that Johm was being held on Stylus.

Suddenly one of Meshet's security rushed into Bubba's office. He told Bubba that Meshet had sent him with a message. "Johm is in space."

"Did Meshet say anything else?" Bubba asked the security officer.

"No Sir." he said. "She said to tell you that and then she fell asleep again."

"Thank you." Bubba said. The security officer left Bubba's office and went back to his duties at Meshet's side.

Bubba quickly made his way to the Comm Room and called Commodore Ail. He told Ail to check the destinations of any ships that left Stylus airspace. There were only three. Bubba ordered Ail to have warships intercept those three ships.

Knowing that he just had to wait for a while Bubba went back to his office. For a little while he just sat behind his desk and looked at his empty coffee mug. Coman got up and filled his fathers mug with fresh coffee and sat it down in front of his father.

"There you go Dad." Coman said sitting the mug on his father's desk.

Finally Bubba looked up. "Thank you Coman." he said but only returned to looking at the mug again. By time Bubba stood the coffee in the mug was cold.

"I can't think right now." Bubba told Coman. "I need to go home … maybe take a nap."

"Okay Dad." Coman said. "I'll take care of things if I can."

When Bubba got home he found the house empty. Sitting on the couch he broke down crying.

"I really need you Father. Only you know where my son is. Please help us to find Johm. Please tell me what to do."

Bubba stood and went to the bedroom where he lay down and took a nap. When he woke up he could hear voices in the house. He got up and walked down the stairs. Becka was in the kitchen.

"Who were you talking to?" Bubba asked his wife.

"She was talking to me Dad." Meshet said from the couch. She was laying on the couch so her father did not see her when he walked by.

"They let you come home?" Bubba asked his daughter. "You looked pretty messed up when I left the hospital."

"I'm okay Dad but have you heard anything about Johm?"

"Nothing." Bubba said. "I went to the palace and then came home."

"At the palace he only looked at his coffee mug so I filled it for him." Coman said as he walked into the den. "Then he stared at it again until the coffee got cold."

"He did not drink the coffee?" Becka asked.

"Not a drop." Coman said.

"You can go to hell for that Dad." Meshet said trying to get her father to laugh.

35

Bubba did not smile. He looked around and seemed to be in his own little world. This was really getting to him.

"Here Baby." Becka said to her husband as she helped him to the couch. "Just sit here and I'll get you some ice tea."

Becka went into the kitchen where she waved for Meshet and Coman to come to her. When they got in the kitchen Becka whispered to them.

"Your father seems to be out of it so I'll need you two to help me with him."

"I think Dad may have lost it." Coman said.

"I'll sit with him." Meshet said. "He likes it when I sit with him."

Meshet walked over to her father. He was looking straight ahead with a blank look on his face.

"Daddy." Meshet said quietly. "Can I sit with you?"

Bubba looked up at Meshet and smiled. "Anytime you want Baby Doll."

Instead of sitting beside her father she sit in his lap. She was short for a hybrid and with her thin frame she weighed almost nothing.

With the smile on his face he said; "I remember holding you and your brother ..." he said before crying again. Later Becka walked her husband to their bedroom and lay him in the bed like she had done so many times before. Then she put on his favorite nightgown and lay beside him. This time she lay on his arm facing him. She held him tight all night.

One time during the night Becka woke up and found Bubba at the desk writing in his diary. On the desk was a fresh hot mug of coffee. She knew that her husband was back.

"Thank you Father for bringing my husband back to me."

Becka fell asleep again and woke up later that morning. She got dressed and walked down to the den. "Where's your dad?" Becka asked Meshet.

"He left for the palace about an hour ago." Meshet said.

"How was he acting?"

36

"Okay I guess." Meshet informed her mom. "He did look a little spaced out though."

"What do you mean ... spaced out?" Becka asked.

"He's okay Mom." Coman said being tired of this conversation.

"Okay ... sorry." Becka said. "I was just worried for your father."

During the night Bubba had received a message from Commodore Ail. Three ships had left Stylus for space taking cargo to the planets Zim and Noter 3. Ail had them stopped and boarded for search. After finding no trace of Johm they were released to continue on their way. There was one cargo ship that was suppose to have gone to the other side of Stylus but it also went into space. This ship could not be found.

"Do you know where or at least which direction the ship went?" Bubba asked Ail from the Comm Room of the palace.

"We think that it headed for the other side of the galaxy Sir." Ail said. "Should I send ships to search out the other side of the galaxy?"

"Let me clear that with Yunnan first." Bubba advised the Commodore. Then he went to Yunnan's office to talk to him about it.

"Good morning." Yunnan said as Bubba walked into the office. "You can take a few days off if you want."

"I need to stay busy Sir." Bubba explained. "I almost lost it yesterday." Then he went on to tell Yunnan about the cargo sip that went to the other side of the galaxy

"Tell Ail to search the other side of the galaxy if you want." Yunnan advised. "Just keep enough ships here to protect Stylus."

"Thank you Sir." Bubba said. Then he went back to the Comm Room and contacted Ail again.

"The King said to go ahead and search the other side of the galaxy for any traces of Johm." Bubba told the Commodore.

"I can send three squadrons and still have over two squadrons left here in Stylus airspace." Ail advised his Prime Minister. "But half a galaxy is a large area to search. We still may find nothing."

"At least try to find my son." Bubba insisted.

"I will Sir." Ail said.

Bubba went back to his office and got back to his duties as Prime Minister. Coman and Lesst were at their desks. Bubba got a mug of coffee and then sat behind his desk.

"You okay Dad?" Lesst asked.

Bubba looked up at his daughter and smiled. "I'm okay."

"You scared us yesterday." Coman said.

"I know and ... I'm sorry for that but ... I'm okay now." Bubba assured them both. "I just need to stay busy."

"Well I have a lot of typing to do if you want to help." Lesst joked.

Bubba smiled again and said; "No thank you. I have plenty here to keep me busy."

Later Bubba, Coman, and Lesst broke for lunch and met Becka in the lunchroom. A few minutes later Yunnan and Yushera came in and got their lunch. Sitting at the table beside Bubba Yushera asked Bubba if he was doing okay.

"Everyone needs to leave Bubba alone." Yunnan insisted. "But what do I know? I'm just the King."

Everyone laughed knowing that Yunnan was just joking around. They talked a little bit but not about Johm. Then they all went back to their offices and back to work.

Three days later Ail called Bubba with a verbal report. The three squadrons had entered the other side of the galaxy and spread out. One of the Superships found a planet with a breathable atmosphere. There were no Zim there but an old ship building site was found. As the Supership left the planet four Zim Superships met the Stylus Supership in space. With the Stylus Supership having three Speargun lasers they quickly destroyed two of the Zim Superships. Receiving damage itself the Stylus Supership left the area. However; the other two Zim Superships fallowed.

Within thirty minutes two other Stylus Superships showed up and attacked the two Zim Superships. Both Zim Superships were destroyed and fifty-nine prisoners were taken. Two Stylus warships came and towed the Zim Superships back to Stylus. The Zim Superships would be repaired and used as Stylus Superships.

Two more warships were sent to where the battle had started to get those two Zim Superships but, when they got there they found three Zim warships already there. Two of them were towing their Superships someplace. The other one opened fire on the Stylus Superships. The Stylus warships left the area towing the Zim warships. The only problem was that if the Stylus warships could see the Zim ships then surely the Zim ships could see them. Ail ordered one of the warships to fallow with the other two following far behind them. Hopefully the Zim warships would not be able to detect the single Stylus warship. It worked.

About three hours later the Zim warships came to another planet with a breathable atmosphere. The Stylus ships hung way back and hid behind a moon of another planet. The name of this planet that the Zim warships flew to was Mesh Ting 2.

Mesh Ting 2 had no intelligent life forms on it but it did have many types of animals including primates. One type of these primates walked upright and showed some intelligents. The Zim used them as slaves for heavy work that needed to be done.

The two Stylus warships came back to Stylus with their captured Zim Superships in tow. The enemy Superships were set down at ship building site and the work on them began that day.

Under Bubba's orders Commodore Ail gathered the Stylus Superships and warships and headed to Mesh Ting 2 to destroy all of the Zim ship building sites and any ships found.

The two squadrons of Stylus Superships and warships met about thirty Zim Superships in space and the battle was on. It was quite the site to watch the large Superships fly between each other with such ease. Over and over they passed an enemy ship firing at it when they passed. This battle lasted just over three hours leaving six Zim Superships and four warships to flee in different directions. Thirty one of the Stylus Superships and two warships survived the battle.

This time seventy three Zim prisoners were taken. The two Stylus warships towed two more Zim Superships back to Stylus for repairs. The Superships towed the rest of the captured Zim ship back to Stylus. Any Stylus Superships that were left patrolled Mesh Ting 2 capturing fifteen more prisoners.

The captured Zim were taken to the POW prison in the desert of Stylus. They were placed in tents until more buildings could be built for them. After two days the Superships patrolling Mesh Ting 2 came home.

Bubba was still not happy. Mesh Ting 2 might have been a Supership building planet but Johm was not there. So where was he?

Chapter 4

Savior of the Zim

Johm woke up in a dark room. He stood and felt around but had no idea where he was. A large steel door opened at the other end of the room. Johm walked out and into another room with bright lights. Looking back he realized that he had been in one of the same containers that the coffee was in.

"Please step this way Johm." a female voice said. He looked around the corner of the container and saw Obi standing there.

"What's going on Obi?" Johm asked.

"I'm sorry that we had to get rough but ... believe it or not ... we saved your life." Obi said.

"And who is We?" Johm asked.

"The Resistance." Obi said. The Stylus government had you targeted for assassination."

"That's right Johm." someone else said. Stogy stepped out of the shadows. "Your own father was going to have you killed."

"Now why would my father do that?" Johm asked.

"You're father considered you an embarrassment to the family and especially Stylus." Obi said. "That is why we had to get you out of there like we did."

"My sister."

"She got drugged the same as you but we left her there." Stogy said. "By now she is probably back home."

Stogy and Obi took Johm to his room on the ship that they were on. They tried in every way to make him feel like he was not a prisoner. Once he was settled in his room. Stogy had a talk with Johm and let him know where he could and could not go on the ship. Then he left Johm and Obi to be alone.

Obi did not really like Johm as her boyfriend. She was

simply a Zim spy doing her job to make Johm feel like she liked him. She was good at her job and had him convinced that she was the woman for him. She went all the way and did what ever was needed to keep him convinced that she was the only female hybrid for him. After a short time Obi left.

For a while Johm stayed in his room alone. Then Obi came to his room again to talk to him. They talked for many hours. By time the ship got to it's destination Obi had Johm convinced that his father really did put out orders to have him eliminated. Johm was primed and ready for a little brainwashing.

"Here we are." Stogy said as he entered Johm's room. "Let's go."

Stogy and Obi lead Johm off of the ship and onto the ground of some planet. He looked around but nothing looked familiar.

"Where are we?" Johm asked anyone listening.

"We're on the planet Prompt 4. This is the hideout for the Resistance Movement.

"Why would the Resistance Movement be based on another planet way out from Stylus?"

"Well ... to be honest ... the Zim have helped us." Obi said. "You are really Zim."

"What do you mean?" Johm asked her.

"You were kidnapped when the Stylus attacked the planet Zim many years ago." Stogy said. "In order to complete the story of the Prophecy Twins your father took you in. Then they told everyone that you and your sister were in fact the Prophecy Twins."

"You and Meshet are exactly the same age but she is not really your sister." Obi added.

"That's why she and I are so different." Johm uttered."

"That's right."

"So what do I do now?" Johm asked.

"We tell the Zim that you are the Prophecy Child and that there was never a Prophecy Twins." Stogy said.

"If you read the Prophecy Text you would see that it mentions a Prophecy Child not twins." Stogy said. "The idea of

Prophecy Twins was a Stylus idea."

"You really are the Prophecy Child but your sister is just another Stylus hybrid." Obi told him.

"That's why we grabbed you but left her there." Stogy added.

"So what do we do now?" Johm asked.

"You fallow me and Obi." Stogy told him. "We will lead you to someone else that will complete your training."

"Okay." Johm said.

Johm was confused. All of his life he was told that he was one of the Prophecy Twins and now he learns that he is the Prophecy Child. There never was a Prophecy Twins. But that did explain how that he and his sister were so different. They were not even brother and sister. Then he started to wonder how many other lies he was told.

Johm spent the rest of the day with Stogy and Obi. They showed him his room in a building that was built to house many of the hybrids working there. Then they showed him a gate marked with red stripes.

Anytime you come to a gate or door with the red stripes just remember that you cannot go in." Stogy informed him.

"Security will not allow you past anyway." Obi added. "But you can walk anyplace else you want."

Then Stogy and Obi took Johm to a Zim monk named Stylum.

"I will be helping you to complete your training as the Prophecy Child." Stylum said. "You will meet me here at 0600 hours tomorrow and … you will not be late."

Stylum quickly turned and went into his room leaving Johm, Stogy, and Obi standing there.

"And he means it too." Obi said. "Don't be late."

"So what's he gon'a do if I am late?" Johm asked.

"Do you like exercising?" Stogy asked.

"I can do it." Johm was full of himself.

"All day long and into the night … nonstop."

"Johm … try to understand." Obi said. "If you do not fallow Stylum's instructions then security will find you and drag you back to him. You have no choice in this. You are the Prophecy Child and you need to finish your training."

Okay okay." Johm said. "I'll do it."

There were many parts involved in Johm's training. The first thing that Stylum had to teach Johm was obedience. Johm had a problem with doing something he was ordered to do but did not want to do. "You must first learn to obey orders. Only then can you give orders." Stylum told him many times. It took longer to teach this to Johm than anyone thought.

Survival tactics was a big part of Johm's training. If he could not survive a situation then what kind of Prophecy Child was he? Hand to hand combat training was the next thing he was taught. He was also taught in what edible plants there were and where to find them; including on which planets they grew. Escape and evasion tactics took up a great deal of time.

Johm got one day a week off from his training and even on that day he was taught the teachings of Muchee in the morning. The name Muchee was the Zim and Stylus name for Jesus.

Each Sunday after his class on the teachings of Muchee Obi would visit him. This was the only time that Johm was allowed contact with others other than his instructor; Stylum.

"Oh it is so good to see you again." Obi told Johm as they hugged each other. She continued to play her roll as his girlfriend.

Obi told Johm the news from Stylus of how that the Prime Minister was having everyone in the Resistance Movement arrested and executed. "Your father had gone quite mad." Obi told him. Of course this was just another lie. Bubba was executing no one.

"That's not like my father." he said.

"He isn't your father Johm … remember?"

"Oh yeah." he said. "I forgot." Then he looked at Obi. "Who are my real parents?"

"We are still trying to find out who they are but we know nothing yet." Obi lied again.

Later Stogy came around and joined the two. He had been

busy unloading a cargo ship. It was hard work but at least it was work. The three walked around for a while.

"What's that over there?" Johm asked.

Johm was pointing at Zim soldiers but Stogy and Obi did not want him to know that. "That's some of the resistance training."

"Then why are you two not there?" Johm asked.

"Our part of the resistance is not doing what they are doing." Obi advised.

"Let's go eat." Stogy suggested. "I'm hungry."

The three walked to the lunch hall where they picked up trays and got their food. Then they sat down together. At the other end of the lunch hall were many of the Zim soldiers.

"So what are they training to attack?" Johm asked.

"Just training to protect everyone here ... that's all." Stogy informed Johm.

"I haven't seen any warships or Superships here." Johm mentioned.

"You won't see any." Obi said.

"In case the Stylus find us we do not want them knowing that Zim soldiers are here." Stogy said. "Therefore ... we will tell them that we all are Zim and Stylus that are tired of the war. They won't find any weapons or any paperwork condemning us."

"What if they find me?" Johm asked.

"They won't find you." Obi insisted with a smile. "I think we need to show him where to run to if Stylus ships do show up." Stogy agreed.

"Just remember that if the Stylus come here it will be only to take you back." Stogy said. "Do you want to go back?"

"No way." Johm said.

Stogy and Obi showed Johm three places that he could run to if he needed to hide. All three hiding spots were spread out so that no matter where Johm was on the compound he would have a place close by to quickly get to.

"Now you remember the places marked in red you're not allowed to go into?" Obi asked. "These hiding places are marked with white stripes."

"You will not see white stripes anyplace else." Stogy added.

"Ha Johm." Stogy stated. "Isn't your birthday tomorrow?"

"I thought you two forgot." Johm said.

"Not at all my friend." Stogy said. "It's getting late so go back to your room and get some rest. We have a party to set up."

Johm went back to his room and lay down with a novel. His mom and sister got him into reading a few novels from Earth. This novel was the first in the *Texas Under Siege* series. Somehow Obi had grabbed the four novels in this series and had them when they abducted Johm. Before long he was fast asleep.

Johm only got up once during the night and finally got up just after four in the morning. He had no training that day because it was his birthday. Actually his not training that day was part of the bigger plan so that Stogy and Obi could continue their part of the brainwashing.

While Johm was in the lunch hall easting breakfast Stogy and Obi joined him. After getting their breakfast they sat across from him at the table.

"Your party awaits you as soon as you finish eating." Stogy said. "This is your day … all day."

As soon as Johm finished his breakfast the three went to a small meeting hall in which tables were set up. A large cake was in the middle of the main table. As they talked friends that Johm had made there walked in for his party. Many of those there did not even know Johm but they played their part in his brainwashing.

Finally Johm was sat in front of the cake as everyone sang the traditional Earth Happy Birthday song. Then they clapped their hands as Johm blew out the eighteen candles. Obi cut the cake into pieces and passed it out to everyone there. Then suddenly the sirens outside began to blow.

Stogy jumped up and yelled; "You all know what to do." Then he looked at Johm and added; "The Stylus are here."

Stogy and Obi grabbed Johm and lead him to a corner of the room and lifted a wooden crate. Under the crate was a tunnel with a ladder that went down. Obi went down first and then Johm and Stogy. Others there lowered the heavy crates to cover the hole.

When the three climbed down about twenty feet they came to another tunnel that went two different directions. Obi lead the way again until they came to small room with three beds and enough stored food to last a long time for three people.

On the surface of Prompt 4 all of the Zim and hybrids hid any weapons that they had. The fighting training camp was changed to look like an exercise area for anyone wanting to stay in good shape. In all ways this looked just like a group of Zim, Stylus, and hybrids trying to avoid the war.

Five Stylus Superships were hovering above the planet with one of them above the camp. No weapons were detected so the Commander of the Supership above the camp transported down to the surface. When the Supership Commander appeared on the surface the leader of the group walked up to him and shook his hand.

"I'm Duffy … the leader of this group." the camp leader said.

I'm Commander Pilk of the Stylus Space Fleet." Pilk said. "We are searching planets for someone."

"Sorry Commander." Duffy said. "We are only peace loving Zim, Stylus, and hybrids trying to stay out of the war. As you can see we do not even have or allow any weapons."

"Well my soldiers will keep their weapons until we finish looking around." Pilk insisted.

"Oh that's fine." Duffy agreed. "May I show you around?"

Commander Pilk sent thirty of his soldiers out among the camp to search for Johm and any weapons. Duffy showed the Commander around the camp as the soldiers searched for Johm. For three hours the soldiers search the camp and found nothing.

"Commander." Duffy said. "Would you like to have dinner with me tonight?"

"Actually … I would love that but the Prime Minister has us looking for his son."

"I don't know much about your Prime Minister." Duffy lied. "I've been here a long time but I think I heard that he is from … Earth is it?"

"That's right." Pilk said. "His son is half human and half Stylus."

"What's his name?" Duffy asked. "If he is here then … well … let's just say that I want no trouble here."

"His name is Johm."

Duffy pretended to think for a moment. "No Johm here but he could have changed his name when he got here."

"Before leaving I would like to satisfy my Prime Minister's mind by telling him that I did see every face that lives here." Pilk said.

"No problem." Duffy said. "When you get ready to leave just let me know and I will call everyone out here for you to look at."

"Found nothing Sir." one of the soldiers told his Commander. "No Johm and not one weapon except for knives in the kitchen."

Pilk looked at Duffy and asked; "Could you call everyone out here now?"

"Yes Sir." Duffy replied and then pushed a button on a device on his wrist. "Attention everyone. This is Duffy. I need everyone out here so the Commander and his men can look at everyone and then get on their way."

It did not take long for every Zim and hybrid to show up except, of course, Stogy, Obi, and Johm. Some of the Zim pretended to be from Stylus. With the Zim and Stylus looking alike who could say anything else? While Commander Pilk looked the members of the camp over his men searched for anyone that might be hiding. The soldiers found no one and Pilk did not find Johm in the crowd.

"Thank you for your cooperation Mister Duffy." Pilk said as his men started transporting back up to the Supership. After talking a few more minutes Commander Pilk transported up to the Supership along with the last few soldiers. As the Superships left Prompt 4 airspace Duffy got back on the mic on his wrist and told everyone that it was safe. However; the Superships can detect anyone from twenty five miles out so Johm would have to stay in hiding for a few more days.

The underground room that Johm was in was not very big but, when Stogy and Obi left it was okay. He took advantage of his being there and got some much needed rest.

Waking up later he dug through some of the food and found a can of stew. Pealing back the top of the can he put the can to his mouth and drank the liquid in the stew and then some of the chunks of meat, potatoes, and carrots. Using his fingers he dug out the last chunk of meat and potato.

Being board he stepped off the room to figure out the size of it. It was about twenty feet long and ten feet wide. That would be a fairly large room but with the three beds and crates of can foods it looked much smaller. Suddenly he heard the heavy wooden crates above the ladder being moved. Someone was coming down.

"It's me Johm." Stogy said as he climbed down the ladder.

"Good to see you … to see anyone." Johm said as Stogy walked over to him.

"I know it's boring down here so I brought your books." Stogy said. "Now you have something to read."

"What's going on up there?" Johm asked.

"The Stylus may be gone but they can still come back." Stogy told Johm. "We just need to make sure that they are not up there still looking down here for you."

"How much longer will I be down here?"

"That's up to Duffy." Stogy replied. "He is the boss here."

After a few more minutes Stogy left. Johm lay on his bed and opened his novel and started reading again. Finally he fell asleep again.

Around noon Obi came down to Johm and told him that he could come out. He wasted no time climbing the ladder and taking in a deep breath of air.

"Oh Muchee that feels good." Johm said.

"The air down there is recycled from up here." Obi told him. "You had fresh air down there."

"Maybe I just don't like being cooped up." Johm tried to explain.

"What do you mean by ... cooped up?"

"That's an expression from Earth meaning being locked up." Johm explained. "My dad used to use it all the time."

"Remember Johm." Obi told him. "He is not your dad. We still have not found out who is but we know that the Prime Minister of Stylus is not your father."

"I forgot." Johm said not sure if Obi was telling him the truth.

"Then why do I have such a strong felling for him if he is not my father?"

"Because he did raise you but he is not your biological father.

What Johm was feeling was that ability to sense things that no one else could sense. He and Meshet possessed this ability. However; in Johm's training he was not being taught to use this ability of getting information from just a feeling. The Zim did not want him to improve on this ability or he might not except the Zim as his people.

That night as he lay in his bed he thought about his sister. For a moment he thought he could hear her but opened his eyes and decided that it had to have been a dream. However: it was not a dream.

Far across the light years of space Meshet had contacted her brother for just a split second but, that split second was enough for her.

Chapter 5

A Point in Space

Bubba talked to Yunnan about keeping two squadrons at the abandoned Zim ship building site as a base for recon missions on the other side of the galaxy. Yunnan loved the idea. Because Revis and Lesst were married Bubba did not want to send Revis' 2nd. Squadron there so Ail sent two other squadrons. Bubba also sent two thousand soldiers and construction workers to rebuild the buildings and barracks for the Stylus soldiers.

Almost every day reports came to Meshet's desk for her father. One day she got a report from a young Commander of a Supership on the other side of the galaxy. Commander Pilk had reported that he located a group of Zim, Stylus, and hybrids on the planet named Prompt 4. These people were simply trying to stay out of the war between the Zim and Stylus. After searching the camp no weapons were found and Johm was not found either.

Meshet concentrated and for a split second she thought that she saw her brother. "Dad." she said. "You need to look at this."

Bubba read the report and then looked at Meshet. "We find these all of the time." he said. "We don't bother them but we do watch them."

"No Dad." Meshet said. "I just tried to communicate with Johm and for just a second I saw him." Meshet stepped over to her father's desk. "Johm is there Dad."

Bubba looked into his daughter's eyes and then asked; "Are you sure?"

"I thought about this camp on Prompt 4 and then tried to contact Johm." she said. "I saw him but I cannot promise that he is there."

Bubba stood and walked into the Comm Room. Then he contacted Commander Pilk and told the Commander what he thought.

"I can be back there in a few hours Sir." Pilk suggested.

"Do it Commander." Bubba ordered. "But do not wreck the place. We do not want to make enemies of these people. Tell this ... Duffy that your coming back is just a routine check."

"Yes Sir." Pilk said and then ordered his ship and the four Superships with him to turn and go back to Prompt 4.

Bubba walked back into his office and told Meshet what he did. "Keep trying to contact your brother."

"Okay Dad." Meshet said as she got back to her work. From time to time she would try contacting Johm again but she got nothing.

Commander Pilk turned his five Superships around and headed back to Prompt 4. Within three hours all five Superships hovered above the camp on Prompt 4. Before they got to the planet the Zim sensors detected the Stylus Superships and the alarm went off again. This time Johm went into the hiding place by himself.

Again Commander Pilk had the crew look for any weapons but again, they found none. This time Pilk had armed soldiers transport down the surface first. When they told him that it was clear the Commander also transported down.

"Mister Duffy." Pilk said as he stuck out his hand. The two men shook hands.

"Commander ... Pilk is it?" Duffy pretended to not remember.

"Yes Sir it is." Pilk said. "We are just coming through this area and stopped to look around again."

"No problem Commander." Duffy said. "Just keep your war out there in space and not here."

"Is there anything that we could help you with?" Pilk asked. Our Prime Minister likes those of you that are embracing the ... how can I call it?"

"The lack of war?" Duffy asked."

"That will work." Pilk said. "Actually ... I am tired of it

52

too."

"There is one thing that you could help us with." Duffy said. "The first of us ... including myself ... crashed here on two Zim cargo ships. We are repairing those ships so we can use them around here."

"What about them?"

"Well ... after we get them flying again do you think that you can keep from shooting them down when you come again?" Duffy asked.

"As long as they are not armed then I wouldn't care." Pilk assured Duffy.

"Thank you Commander." Duffy said. "The cargo ships will help us move things around."

"Why do you need two of them?" Pilk asked.

"We were also thinking of going into the mountains to look for precious metals and stones. If we find any then maybe we can trade with Stylus."

"That's a good idea." Pilk agreed. "Good luck in your mining."

A soldier walked up to Pilk and whispered in his ear. "Nothing Sir."

"Well I really need to go Mister Duffy." Pilk said. "They keep me running."

"Maybe next time you can stay a while." Duffy mentioned. "Maybe your crew can use a little time off."

"I'll think it over and thanks for the offer." Pilk said.

Commander Pilk called his soldiers together and had them transport up with him being the last to leave the surface. Then the five Superships left Prompt 4 airspace.

This time Johm spent three days in the hole. It was a different hole than he had been in the first time but almost looked the same. This hole had only one bed and there were more crates of canned food stacked in the far corner. Like the other hole it was about twenty feet by ten feet but the ceiling was only about six and a half feet tall. The first hole had a higher ceiling. Johm lay down to wait as long as he had to.

As the hours passed Johm found that one of the crates had

bottled water. He ate some more stew although he had no idea what animal the meat was from. With no way to tell the time the days ran into the nights and time seemed to stop. Finally Stogy came down one day and brought him out of the hole.

"Sorry but that Stylus ship kept hanging around." Stogy said. "But I have good news."

"What's that?" Johm asked.

"We have permission from the Stylus ship Commander to repair two cargo ships." Stogy informed Johm. "Stylum has been moved to a cave in the mountains far from here. We will be moving you there as well."

"When?"

"In about an hour." Stogy advised. "Get your things together."

Johm went to his room and gathered his things. There was not much to get. He did remember his notes from classes with Stylum and his novel. One of the cargo ships came in and landed in the middle of the camp. Johm climbed on board along with a few other miners with some cargo. The door closed and the ship lifted off.

The cargo ship flew for almost an hour and landed close to the mouth of a cave. The miners rushed Johm off of the ship and into the cave where Stylum met him. Then they went back and brought some of the cargo into the cave. It was food and water for Stylum and Johm. Then the cargo ship lifted off again and flew far off in the distance to where they were to work.

Stylum got right to training Johm. No time was wasted as Johm was already many days behind in his training. Stylum started Johm off with many hours of meditation where Johm would sit or lay still. During this time he would try to block out any noises that kept him from concentrating on his training. Stylum did not make it easy as he sometimes intentionally dropped something or in another way made noises.

This meditation training went on for over a week. The only person that Johm had seen was Stylum. He was beginning to miss Obi and even Stogy. When he mentioned this to Stylum he was ordered to meditate even more.

"Everything ... every thought or desire can be controlled by simply meditating." Stylum said. "You must convince yourself that you can do without that things you desire the most."

"But you don't know Obi." Johm told his instructor.

"I do know Obi and you can do without her." Stylum insisted. "Now convince yourself of that. Meditate on it."

What neither Johm nor Stylum knew was that the more Johm meditated the more his sister was picking up his thoughts.

Back on Stylus Meshet had been picking up flashes of her brother's thoughts for about a week. She could not control it but every once in a while Johm's thoughts would flash through her head. Through the different flashes she put together that he was in a dark cave with some lighting. Sometimes she saw flashes of Obi's and Stogy's faces but still could not tell where he was. Many nights she fell asleep crying. Then finally one night before falling asleep she prayed.

"Muchee ... you're the same as what my father calls Jesus and your father is his god and my god. Please help me to find my brother. I sense a fear in him. Please help him in what ever he is going through. I love my brother. Please help him."

The next morning Meshet got another flash of her brother's thoughts. She saw the face of either a older Zim or Stylus male but the face could be an enemy or friend. She had no way of knowing. Then the word *Zim* kept coming to her mind.

"He's among the Zim." Meshet told her mother and father as she sat down for breakfast.

"As a prisoner or friend?" Becka asked.

Meshet thought for a moment and then said; "He isn't scared so I'm saying ... he is with friends."

"So the question is ... does he know he is among the Zim or has he willingly joined the Zim?" Bubba asked.

"Remember that he is very rebellious right now." Meshet reminded them.

After eating Bubba and Meshet wet straight to Yunnan's office to talk with him about what Meshet was picking up from her brother.

"There you two are." Yunnan said as Bubba and Meshet walked into his office.

Bubba waved his hand and pointed at Yunnan. "Tell Yunnan what you saw."

Meshet told Yunnan everything that she had been seeing and feeling that had to do with Johm. Yunnan sat back in his chair and looked down at the paperwork on his desk.

"So he's crossed over to the other side." Yunnan said. "I never thought that he would go that far."

"We aren't sure Sir." Meshet said. "I just know that he is among the Zim ... maybe a prisoner."

"Do you think they could be holding him for a ransom?" Yunnan asked."

"I don't think so." Bubba said as he rubbed his chin. "If that was their goal then they would have taken Meshet as well."

"Well!" Yunnan said. "Just let me know if there is anything I can do."

"Thank you Sir." Bubba said as he and Meshet left Yunnan's office. "Bubba." Yunnan said just as Bubba and Meshet started to leave his office. "How many times has that camp been searched?"

"At least two times and the Commander said that his soldiers did a very extensive search both times."

"It was just an idea." Yunnan said. "Thank you."

Bubba and Meshet went to the lunchroom to get something to eat. The cook was starting to experiment with different things. The Stylus people loved a version of sauerkraut. On this day he added some sliced ova sausage to the sauerkraut. Bubba got his large bowl that a friend had given him and filled it with the Ova sausage and sauerkraut. When he sat at the table Meshet shook her head from side to side.

"What?" Bubba asked Meshet.

"You're bigger than all Stylus and many of the hybrids so we all know that you eat more but ..." Meshet said but stopped talking not wanting to finish saying what she was thinking."

"But what?" Bubba asked not really expecting an answer.

After eating Bubba went to the Comm Room and contacted Commander Pilk.

"The King asked me how many times you have searched the camp on Prompt 4 so I told him what you told me." Bubba said. "But are you sure you searched the camp real good?"

"Oh yes Sir." the Commander said. "My soldiers said that they moved everything that could be moved and looked behind and under it."

"Okay." Bubba said. "Thank you."

"You're welcome Prime Minister." Commander Pilk said.

Bubba walked back to his office. Meshet had already got back to doing her work. As Bubba sat in his chair something flashed through Meshet's mind again. This time she saw her brother's friend and his girlfriend. Her brother was looking at Stogy and Obi. Then she saw him get on a cargo ship and fly away. But where was he?

"Dad." Meshet said to her father. "I saw him again and this time he was looking at Stogy and Obi."

"Where was he?" Bubba asked.

"I don't know." Meshet answered. "But he got into a cargo ship with a few others. Most of the others were hybrids but some were Stylus ... or Zim."

That was all that Meshet saw and she still did not know where Johm was. That evening at the evening meal in the palace everyone was talking except for Meshet. Her father was not saying much but at least he was talking. Meshet was off in her own little world. From time to time she would stop eating as she saw what her brother was seeing. She seemed to be daydreaming.

After the meal Bubba, Becka, Coman, and Meshet walked up to the house where Bubba got him a mug of hot cocoa and went out on the porch. Sitting in his chair at the table he looked up at the stars.

"Where are you Son?" Bubba whispered not knowing that Meshet was standing there.

"He's ... over there." Meshet said as she pointed into the sky. "I don't know exactly where but ... he is in that direction."

Bubba was depressed. Now that he knew in what direction his son was he still did not know where he was. He had a restless night that night waking up many times after having dreams of his son. Over and over during the night he went back out on the porch and looked up in the direction that Meshet had pointed. He knew that as the planet rotated that point in space moved so, he no longer was looking exactly where his daughter had pointed. Now he did not even know the direction in which his son was.

The next morning Bubba contacted the observatory on the top of a mountain about one hundred miles away. He told the head scientist there what his daughter had told him the night before and asked the scientist if he could figure out the direction that Meshet had pointed. The scientist asked Bubba a few questions such as the angle in which Meshet pointed and what time she did the pointing. Then he told his Prime Minister that he would figure it out and contact Bubba later with a line of direction. Bubba was happy.

Bubba then went to his office and told Meshet what he had done. She would need to let her father know when the scientist called back.

Bubba was still having problems with group of Stylus that wanted all firearms taken from the public. Over the past few years crime had climbed and even tripled. Just twenty years earlier there was hardly any crime at all and now the government was having to build hundreds of city jails and prisons.

Then one day Rommin came into Bubba's office. They had not seen each other for quite a while.

"I have almost twenty thousand POW's in my prison's." Rommin said. "Some of them I trust ... and ... you need help on cleaning up after the Zim attack many years ago. I am suggesting that we use some of the POW's for work in that cleaning up and in some of the mines.

"I like using the rock quarry for local punishment but we do have a few mineral mines in the mountains that need miners." Bubba advised.

Rommin got right to finding POW's to work the mines. This also opened more jobs for security and POW transportation. The three gremite mines were located far away from the POW prison. One was on the other side of the planet. Prisons near these mines needed to be built and security measures needed to be set up such as fences, food storage and other things.

Rommin decided to have the prisoners live in tents as they had before and build the prisons needed to house themselves. Then the POW's could move into the prisons and start working the mines. Gremite was used in the particle cannon so Stylus needed it.

A new class of Stylus spies were about to graduate. Bubba wanted all seven of them to infiltrate the local resistance movement in hopes of finding Johm. Three of them tried joining the local resistance group that Stogy and Obi was a part of.

With Stogy and Obi gone another Stylus was in charge of the local resistance movement but he was a dangerous person. His name was Stumb. Stumb was an excessively mean and rebellious Stylus that stayed in trouble with the law all of the time. He had been in trouble with the local law ever since he was six years old when he stabbed his teacher with a pencil.

Stumb was even mean to the other members of the resistance. He got so bad at one point that Stogy had to have a talk with him. But with Stogy no longer there he could do what ever he wanted.

One evening Stumb and a few of the other resistance members attacked the local police department. They started by throwing rocks through the front windows of the department. As the police ran out to catch who was throwing the rocks Stumb opened fire with a pistol that the others did not know he had. He killed two of the police officers and wounded another one. Then as the other resistance members ran Stumb shot two of them.

The plan was to just break the windows and maybe throw a few rocks at the cops but that was all. When Stumb shot the cops the others ran not wanting to be a part of any murders. Stumb yelled out calling them cowards and shot two of them. One of them died later.

Some of the police outside stopped Stumb's rampage by shooting him. He was rolled over and his hands were cuffed behind him. He continued to yell cursing the police until he finally died of his wounds.

Stumb was just one example of how the young Stylus had changed over the past twenty years. There was no police department twenty years earlier because there was no need for any police. And now police were being killed every now and then. These were not the first police killed in the line of duty and they would not be the last.

Angered over the rash of police being killed Bubba wrote out another bill making it an executional offence for anyone found guilty of killing a police officer. Then he walked the bill into Yunnan's office and explained the bill. Yunnan did not even think about it and signed the bill into law. From then on anyone arrested for killing a police officer was given one appeal and that was all. If still found guilty they were executed the next day by hanging.

Over the next month five men and one woman was hung for murdering police officers. They were all young Stylus under the age of twenty-two with four of them being hybrids. All six were found to be members of the resistance movement.

Bubba got the call from the scientist at the observatory. Not being sure exactly where Meshet had pointed the scientist came up with a ling through space. Meshet had to have pointed someplace along that line. Unfortunately; that entire line was through the middle of the galaxy. There was no way to pinpoint any single spot.

Chapter 6

The Disciple

The three spies joined the resistance movement that Stogy was in. Luckily they joined after the incident at the police department. Not long after joining they heard about the camp on Prompt 4. After realizing that Johm was not there on Stylus they tried to get moved to Prompt 4.

Two of the spies were close to the age of forty so the new leader of the movement did not trust them. However; the third one was a nineteen year old hybrid. He was put on a cargo ship delivering mining supplies to the miners on Prompt 4. The miners had discover large pockets of precious stones. Using these stones they bought mining supplies to help them in their mining.

After dropping off their cargo at the mine the cargo ship lifted off and took the young spy to the camp. They also had cargo for the camp as well.

The young spy's name was Routen. He was a nineteen year old hybrid with one mission; to blend into the population of Prompt 4 and find Johm. He had been trained in security hoping that his training might help him to get closer to information about those in the area. Being able to go to Prompt 4 was an extra.

By time Routen got to Prompt 4 the other two spies had already got word to Prime Minister Bubba about the younger one going to Prompt 4. Bubba could not have been happier.

Routen knew what Johm looked like and watched carefully for him. With his training in security he was placed at one of the gates marked in red. When he asked about the red stripe he was only told that most of those there were not allowed to enter that area. He was not even allowed to enter. For now he would take his time and allow time for his supervisors to get used to and start trusting him. That took time.

Over the next month Routen paid attention and listened. Finally he heard talk of a hybrid that lived in a cave with an older Zim that was teaching him. The problem was what was he teaching Johm?

The next time that Commander Pilk came around he had his men search the camp as usual. The Commander walked around with Duffy and shook hands with many of the workers. When they came to Routen standing duty at the gate Pilk shook his hand. That was when Routen slipped a note into Pilk's hand with the handshake. Pilk quickly slid his hand into his pants pocket and released the note there.

Later Commander Pilk and his men left. As the Superships lifted off Pilk took the note out of his pocket. He already knew that a spy was in the camp and that his name was Routen.

> I am Routen. Johm may be at cave
> located about 100 miles north of
> this camp. He is with older Zim
> teaching him something. From
> now on search under my bed for
> other notes.

Commander Pilk turned his ships northward and looked for a cave in which Johm might be in. They searched many caves and finally came to the mine where the miners were working. Calling all of the miners out to look at them Pilk realized that Johm was not there.

Coincidentally; Johm and Stylum had come into the camp just before the five Superships arrived. Routen had no way of knowing this. The alarm went off when the Superships arrived and Johm and Stylum went into hiding. When the alarm sounded the "all clear" they came out of their hole. Duffy, Obi, and Stogy met them. Playing her part Obi ran into Johm's arms.

"That was close." Stylum said. "Why are they coming

around so much?"

"I think they suspect something." Stogy admitted.

"We need to get him out'a here." Obi suggested.

"Wait a minute." Duffy said. "We can't move him."

"Why not?" Obi asked.

"Anything we do with Johm needs planning." Duffy advised. "We need to have a meeting and decide what to do."

"Am I going to be invited to this meeting that involves me?" Johm asked.

"Of course. Duffy said not wanting to tell him no. Johm had no say so in what their plans were but he could not tell Johm that.

Under Duffy's orders Johm and Stylum were taken back to the cave where workers made a hiding area in the back of the cave for Johm and Stylus. Then they worked on the mouth of the cave to make it look like another mine. There were no precious minerals or stones there but they made it look good anyway. Within six days the workers were finished. The cave looked Ikea working mine.

A cargo ship took all but three of the workers back to the camp. Those three stayed behind to make Stylum's cave look like a working mine of some type. This was needed in case the Commander came back and; they knew that he would.

Prompt 4 had been a dead planet for over a million years. That estimation came from test done many years earlier but before that one million years was unknown. So it was shocking when the three hybrid miners found coal. Coal came from very large decayed animals millions of years earlier. Therefore there had to be gas and oil as well. Diamonds came from coal so were there diamonds someplace?

When Duffy got this news he got excited. Things were starting to look up for those on Prompt 4. Duffy declared that anyone wishing to do so may claim up to half a mile of land for a personal mine that they and their family could work. The mine did not have to produce anything special but the land was still owned by the person making the claim. However; this almost became Duffy's undoing.

Many of those living in the camp that also supplied services to the camp were leaving and going into the mountains to claim their hopes of fortune. However; this was good news for those like Routen who was hired by one of the more profitable miners for security at his mine.

With luck on Routen's side Johm was being moved from mine to mine to keep him hidden from Commander Pilk.

Johm and Meshet were now nineteen years old and Johm's training was almost finished. He had come a long ways but still had spurts of his old self coming out every now and then. For the most part he was already a well adjusted and self controlled man; a true leader of the Zim.

Routen had been hired by a single man that liked his dedication to his work. The hybrid claimed a piece of land where he had found a few precious stones and within a few months was able to hire Routen as Head of Security. Although Routen saw his duty as a spy seriously he saw no reason not to make some money as well. After all; it was just part of his investigation; right?"

Even Commander Pilk was making a few kick-backs of his own. This was not against any laws as long as the gifts were not bribes for overlooking wrong doings. A miner simply showed his appreciation for delivering supplies with a handshake. Of course the miner had something in his hand when he shook the Commander's hand but that was becoming normal.

One precious stone here and there with a handshake was the usual "gift" to the Commander. One miner handed over a small chunk of coal with his handshake. Knowing that the miner was a coal miner Pilk looked at his hand and saw the coal. Then he looked up at the miner who was laughing. The miner joked around all of the time. Not having any precious stones he did treat Pilk to a great meal. That was good enough.

Pilk did take one piece of coal to show the young ones in his family what man on Earth used to use for supplying heat in their homes. The stories he told of the coal were very educational to the young ones.

One day Routen was walking Commander Pilk around

when he handed him another note. It simply read;

Nothing new. Only know that Johm is on
this planet. Good luck.

When Pilk was alone and able to read the note he was depressed. He had to tell his Prime Minister the bad news again. After over a year of searching Prompt 4 his son was still not found. He enjoyed the money he was making from the miners and did not want his Prime Minister to transfer him someplace else. He was quickly becoming a rich man but still had a ways to go before actually being rich. By hiding his intake from the miners on Stylus, every time he went back to Stylus no one knew what all he had.

For the first time Commander Pilk considered lying to his Prime Minister. Greed was now controlling him. Getting richer had become more important than loyalty and devotion. Commander Pilk decided to send the message back to his Prime Minister that Johm was not located yet but he was still on Prompt 4.

Pilk knew he was okay when he received a message back from the Prime minister saying; "Well done. Please continue looking."

Bubba decided to send workers to build a base of operations on Prompt 4. While the base was being built two thousand soldiers would be sent to build a temporary base beside the camp. This temporary base consisted of tents of all sizes. Large tents were set up to hold supplies and showers for the soldiers. Although the planet was mostly a cool desert there was plenty of water below the surface so one drilling rig was set up. Within a week there was plenty of water for the soldiers and the civilians in the neighboring camp.

Duffy did not like the soldiers being right beside his camp but before long other businesses started popping up. Even some of the soldiers opened small businesses like bakers and blacksmiths. Their businesses were open only when they were not on duty. Trading with the miners picked up and everyone was getting their share of the riches.

During all of this Duffy tried to stay in control. If at any time he lost control he would start loosing money. He was already a rich man but greed was controlling him as much as it was controlling Commander Pilk.

Of course with all of the riches flying around crime started taking hold. Routen and his four security officers now carried rifles as well as pistols. Criminals would come into a mine as workers and then force the miner to turn over his mine to them or die. The miner that Routen worked for talked to Commander Pilk about getting better weapons; military weapons to protect his mine.

With greed already taking hold on Commander Pilk he saw a new way to increase his riches. He sold military weapons to a few of the miners but held them to secrecy. No one was to know where the weapons came from. But as resistance against crime went up organized crime started. Before long miners on Prompt 4 were being faced with armed soldiers; large groups of men and women, Zim and hybrids, fighting to take their mines.

Finally Commander Pilk saw what he had created. He knew that he had to do something about this before the Prime Minister found out. He had no control over the two thousand soldiers on the surface but he did have three hundred soldiers under his command. One of his Superships was mainly a large ship designed to carry a large number of soldiers. It was in any other way still armed just like a regular Supership.

The two thousand soldiers were under the control of a Commander Zub; a cousin of Commodore Zu on Stylus. Zub was a loyal Stylus but quickly came under the power of greed. At first he did not see it as greed but just a way to make more wealth before retirement. He loosely controlled his soldiers and allowed them to make their riches as he did as well.

Commander Pilk asked for Commander Zub's help but could not get it. Unknown to everyone Zub was being paid off by the organizer of the organized crime; Duffy himself.

Seeing all of this Johm could not understand why it was

being allowed to continues. He had finished his training and now walked among the people as one of them although they all knew who he was.

Johm was the leader of his people; the savior of not only the Zim but them all. Johm now had the ability to knock a man over just with the wave of his hand. No one challenged him. Johm did not get a hot head thinking that he was better than anyone else although it was tempting. Stylum had trained him well. But there was still something in the back of his head that told him that something was wrong.

Hundreds of Stylus, Zim, and hybrids came to Prompt 4 every week to find their fortunes. Prompt 4 was sometimes called The Planet of Gold. Most did not find their fortunes and turned to crime in order to survive. The call for more protection of the citizens was overwhelming for Zub so he and Duffy had a talk.

"I am only here ... still in control of my soldiers ... because the Prime Minister thinks that I am fighting against the crime here." Zub said. "He will not keep me here if you keep escalating your attacks on the miners."

"Then what do you suggest?" Duffy asked.

"Back off for a while." Zub said. "I will move some soldiers around and make it look like I am stopping the crime around here against the miners. The miners is all Commander Pilk seems to be worried about."

"So if he keeps getting what the miners give him and he is happy then he will report back to Stylus that everything is okay?" Duffy asked.

"Exactly." Zub advised. "In the meantime dibble in other things that the citizens around here want."

"Like what?" Duffy asked.

"Prostitution, drugs, and ... whatever else they want."

Duffy's eyebrows rolled up. "I like the way you think but ... if I did this then it would come to your soldiers as well. That would be a problem for you."

"And I will deal with it then." Zub assured Duffy.

Duffy thought for a moment and then agreed. "Okay

then." Duffy said. "The attacks on the miners will stop. I'll keep my people employed but using them in other ways."

"There you go." Zub was happy. "But can I make anything off of this?"

"Why not." Duffy said. Then he walked over to a safe in his wall and opened it. Then he closed the door to the safe and spun the tumbler. "I love those old safes." he said as he handed Zub a few precious stones. "Don't ask for anymore. I'll pay you from time to time."

"You're the boss." Zub said not realizing what he had said. Duffy was quick to remind him though.

"You remember that." Duffy reminded his new business partner. "I call all of the shots."

Zub then realized what he was into. He no longer called the shots but to what extent? "Only I tell my soldiers what to do." Zub insisted.

"Yes." Duffy admitted. "You do what your Prime Minister tells your little ass to do. But you remember that I can have you eliminated just as easily as I can hand you a few nice looking stones."

"I know." Zub admitted. "I could eliminate you too you know."

Duffy raised a pistol and said; "Not anymore." Then he pulled the trigger three times killing Commander Sub.

Duffy called three of his men and ordered them to take Zub's body out a few miles from the camp and dump it. "Let the vultures have him."

After no one saw Commander Zub for five days Commander Pilk took over the two thousand soldiers on the ground. Then he placed a Lieutenant Tubs in charge of the ground forces. The Prime Minister agreed with this move.

Lieutenant Tubs was a dedicated soldier and very loyal to his men and officers above him. One day just after taking over he walked through the camp and thought he saw Johm. He had seen Johm's photo many times.

"Johm." Tubs said as he passed the hybrid that looked like Johm.

Johm turned expecting to see someone he knew but realized that he had answered the wrong person. "Did you call me Sir?" he said trying to play dumb.

"Is your name Johm?" Tubs asked.

"No Sir." Johm insisted. "I'm Stim."

"I'm sorry Sir." Tubs apologized. "You looked familiar."

"That's okay." Johm said but quickly turned and walked away.

Tubs walked over to Routen standing a little ways away. Routen was in the camp buying some personal supplies for himself and his security.

"Does that hybrid look like Johm to you?" Tubs asked Routen.

"I think so Sir but he has a beard so it's hard to say." Routen said. Zim and Stylus could not grow facial hair but many hybrids could because of the human DNA in them.

"Keep an eye on him." Tubs asked.

"I've heard that he was the savior of the people but that is all." Routen said. "Isn't that what the Stylus called the Prophecy Twins?"

"I'll report this to the Prime Minister."

"Yes Sir." Routen said as Tubs walked away.

Later Johm walked by Routen again so Routen took advantage of it and stuck up a conversation with him.

"Sir." Routen said. "I see you a lot but don't know who you are."

"I seem to be the only one here not wanting to get rich." Johm said with a smile.

"You don't care to get rich?" Routen asked.

"I am full of joy." Johm said. "I am richer than you will ever be."

"You talk like a holy man … a believer in Muchee." Routen said.

"Muchee does guide me through life." Johm admitted. "But greed guides almost everyone else around here."

"I can see that." Routen replied.

"You have taken advantage of some of the wealth but you

have not allowed it to destroy you." Johm mentioned.

"I am also a Mucheeian." Routen admitted. "My parents raised me well."

"Sounds like you have great parents." Johm said.

"What about your parents?" Routen asked Johm.

Johm thought for a while and then asked; "Why are you so interested in my life?"

"I'm sorry Sir." Routen quickly said. "I was just wondering …"

"No you were not just wondering." Johm interrupted Routen. "You are a spy for Stylus."

"How do you know that?" Routen asked scared of being found out. "Can you read my mind or something?"

"Or something is more like it." Johm said. "Your thought scream out for anyone to read."

Routen stood still looking down. "How can I learn to … control my thoughts?"

"It's simple Routen." Give up your riches and fallow me. I will teach you the ways of Muchee … so many things you never knew."

"I would be your disciple?"

"No." Johm quickly corrected Routen. "You would be a disciple of Muchee. I will only be your teacher."

Routen gave the money he had to some of the poor in the camp and then fallowed Johm. As they walked Johm asked Routen how far he would go for him and Muchee. Then he told Routen that he was a wanted man but not for doing anything wrong. He asked Routen if he would keep that secret.

"Of courser I will." Routen insisted. Only then did Johm tell Routen who he really was.

"My father on Stylus wants to silence me but I cannot be silenced."

"But aren't you one of the Prophecy Twins?" Routen asked. "You have a sister."

"I have a step-sister that is not of my blood." John told his follower. "The true prophecy talks about a Prophecy Child not Prophecy Twins. I am that Prophecy Child."

"So what do we do now?" Routen asked.

"We spread the teachings of Muchee until I am called to do what I must do."

"And what is it that you must do?" Routen asked.

"I am not the religious savior of the people." Johm advised. "I am the political savior of the Zim."

"But I am not Zim." Routen mentioned. "I am Stylus."

"I know that." Johm said. "Will you still fallow me?"

Mesmerized with Johm's words Routen agreed to fallow Johm. It no longer mattered what Commander Pilk or the Prime Minister wanted. He had found a much higher calling.

Chapter 7

Holy Man or Savior

Johm and Routen walked from camp to camp on Prompt 4 delivering the messages of Muchee. Being a Holy Man was a good cover for Johm and his real goal. As he worked his way from mining camp to mining camp he watched and listened. Then he realized what he needed to do.

One day Johm was at one of the mining camps when he overheard someone mention that their cargo ship was on it's way to the planet Zim. Zim had been under Stylus control for many years and Johm saw his chance to fulfill the prophecy. He would go to Zim and lead the people of that planet into freedom from their oppression.

After talking to the captain of the cargo ship Johm got permission for him and Routen to go with them. Before leaving Johm spoke one last time to the miners there and won another disciple. Finally Johm and his two disciples were on their way to the planet Zim to fulfill the prophecy of the Prophecy Child.

Meshet had also finished her training. She spent half of her time training as the leader of the Stylus people and the other half of her time working as her father's secretary. Being the Prime Minister's secretary was as demanding as her training but she did it well.

Unlike her brother Meshet did not take on the roll of some type of religious Guru. Then again she did not have to hide like he did. She got a message from Commander Pilk one day that he and Lieutenant Tubs' soldiers had covered every mining camp and settlement there on Prompt 4 and Johm was not found. Then he reported that he heard that Johm and a few disciples were on their way to the planet Zim.

"Zim." Meshet said as she handed the report to her father. "Why is he headed to Zim?"

Bubba read the report and then dropped the message on his desk being disgusted with what he read. "What is that boy doing?"

Bubba went to the Comm Room and contacted Commodore Ail. "I want that cargo ship stopped and Johm arrested." Bubba insisted. "Then I want him brought here."

"Will do Prime Minister." Ail agreed and then quickly contacted Commander Mat who with five Superships patrolled the Zim airspace. But by that time the cargo ship had already dropped off it's cargo for the soldiers as well as Johm and his two disciples.

Commander Mat reported back to Commodore Ail who reported to the Prime Minister that the cargo ship was stopped as it left Zim airspace. The captain of the cargo ship said that he had three passengers which he dropped off with the cargo. Stylus soldiers on Zim reported that the three passengers had already disappeared into the population.

Bubba ordered the soldiers on Zim to search for his son but it was to late. However; the search for Johm would continue and not stop until Johm was found and arrested. The charge would be treason but that was just so that the soldiers would have a reason to arrest Johm.

For a while Johm would not let the Zim know who he was. He and his disciples would spread the teachings of Muchee and get the people to know him. He embraced the roll as a Holy Man as it was a good cover for his real reason for being there. Before long Johm was known around the planet but this caused him to go into hiding.

Each night Johm and his growing number of disciples had to find a place to sleep. But this became a declining problem as his popularity grew. Once a Zim in any given area knew who he was they offered all of them food, water, and a place to rest.

One morning after leaving one man's home Johm came across a woman that was having problems walking. She was headed the same direction as they were. He stopped a man on a cart being pulled by a large animal called a Bocka.

"Sir." Johm yelled out to the man on the cart. The man

73

stopped. "Could you allow this old woman to ride in your cart to the next town?"

"Why should I?" the man asked sharply.

"Remember the teachings of Muchee." Johm said. "Respect your elders and help them for someday you too will be old and in need of help."

The man took in a deep breath and then let it out in a heavy sigh. "Oh … okay but you load her on."

Johm's disciples loaded the old woman on the back of the man's cart and made sure that she would not fall out. "Thank you my Goodman." Johm said to the man on the cart.

The man looked at Johm as if he was crazy. "Who are you?"

"Just a man teaching the ways of Muchee."

"But I don't believe in Muchee." the man insisted.

"And why not?" Johm asked as his disciples just listened and learned.

"I just can't believe in one almighty god that helps us all." the man said. "If that is true then where is my help?"

"But it isn't true." Johm advised the man. "God does not help everyone."

"I know." the man continued.

"Maybe if you were to give Muchee what he wants then he would help you some as well."

"What do you mean?"

"Look at it this way." Johm suggested. "If you keep talking to me like I am an animal then why should I help you in something you want?"

"Get that old woman off of my cart." the man ordered. "Help her yourself."

"You're missing the point my friend." Johm explained. "Why should you help me if I am mean to you or … I just don't give you anything you want?"

The man thought for a moment. "Who are you?" he asked again.

"I am Johm … the Prophecy Child that your mother told you about." Johm admitted not being sure that he should have.

74

"I am the one that has come to save the Zim people from their Stylus oppressors."

"How can I learn the teachings of Muchee?" the man asked.

"Go into the camp ahead and sell your cart." Johm said. "Then find us a place to rest tonight and then join me in my travels."

"Sell my cart?" the man asked. Then something came over him and he changed his mind. "Yes. I'll do that."

Then the man left Johm and his disciples and went to the next town which was a mining camp. He not only dropped off the old woman but helped her into her home. Then he sold his cart, Bocka, and everything in the cart. After talking to a few of those in the camp he mentioned Johm's name. A silence set over the small crowd in the room.

"We heard that a man named Johm was heading this way but is this really the Prophecy Child that we have heard about?" a woman yelled from the back of the room.

The man thought for a moment. "I don't know if he is this Prophecy Child but ... when the man speaks ... well ... you just have to listen to him."

"When will he be here?" the woman asked.

"He's on his way and should be here soon." the man advised. "He and his disciples will need food and a place to rest tonight."

The man made a deal with those there that if Johm spoke a good message then they would set him and his disciples up with all the food and water they could handle as well as a place to sleep that night. Then he went out in the center of the camp and waited for Johm to walk in.

Johm and his two disciples continued to walk towards the mining camp where they had a place to sleep that night waiting for them. As they continued their walk they met with others going the same direction. Johm quickly drew a crowd as he taught them.

"I'm going from town to town to help the men with their love lives." a young hybrid female told Johm. "Why should you care if I am a prostitute?"

"It's really none of my business my lady ..."

"That's right." The woman said laughing. "It is none of your business."

"It's also none of my business if you go to hell either." Johm said. The crowd got quiet.

"Now how can you say that I would go to hell?" the woman yelled.

"Before you do something ask yourself ... would Muchee do this or that." Then he stopped walking and faced the woman. "You should never sleep with another man except for your husband. If you sleep with any other man then you are a sinner and you're going to hell." Johm turned again and continued walking.

Johm continued to teach until he walked into the small town. The man that had sold his cart joined Johm as his third disciple. Johm went into the home of the miner that owned the mine just outside the town. There he and his disciples rested until late that evening. Then in the cool of the setting sun Johm came out to the center of the town and taught the teachings of Muchee.

"Are you this Prophecy Child that we have heard of?" someone yelled out.

"My name is Johm." Johm said with a smile. "I am the Prophecy Child."

"Why should we believe that you are the Prophecy Child?" a man in the crowd yelled out.

"You don't have to believe if you wish not to." Johm told them all. "Let my actions and words tell you who I am."

"But you seem to be some kind of Holy Man ... not a leader that will deliver us from the Stylus."

"Let me say this again." Johm decided to go ahead and allow them to know exactly who he was. "I am Johm ... your Prophecy Child. I will deliver you out of the hands of your oppressors ... the Stylus."

"How can I know that you are who you say you are?" someone else asked.

"Like I have already said … let my actions and words tell you who I am."

"But you have no army."

"An army must be raised. That is true." Johm said. "This new war will not be fought by just the young. It will take all of us."

Suddenly Stylus soldiers rushed in and grabbed Johm. A young Lieutenant said; "You're under arrest for inciting a riot."

For the first time Johm panicked. "Don't allow them to take me away. This war starts now … with you."

A rock was thrown at the soldiers and then another and another. When the crowd saw that the soldiers still held onto Johm they rushed them. With the soldiers having to fight off the mob Johm was able to escape back into the miner's home. Then someone rushed him and his disciples out the back door and down the street. A few minutes later they entered another home.

After hearing shots being fired into the air the crowd left the soldiers alone. Running into every open door and runway between buildings the center of town was quickly emptied. As the soldiers looked around they realized that Johm had slipped away.

Commodore Ail had to pass the report on to his Prime Minister but this report had to be verbal not written. He placed a call to the palace Comm Room and asked for the Prime Minister. A couple of minutes later Bubba was in the Comm Room.

"Commodore Ail." Bubba said with a smile. "How may I help you?"

"I am afraid that I have a bad report for you Sir." Ail said. "Soldiers on Zim grabbed Johm but the civilians started throwing rocks and fighting them. After firing a few shots into the air the crowd vanished but Johm could not be found."

"Is Johm still in that town?" Bubba asked.

"Yes Sir. Ail insisted. "The Lieutenant in charge has surrounded the town and no one is allowed in or out of the town until he hears from me."

"Tell that Lieutenant that he did a great job and send as many solders to him as he needs." Bubba ordered Ail. "Place that town under marshal law and send patrols through the streets every night arresting anyone that they find outside."

"Yes Sir." Ail agreed.

"And one more thing Commodore."

"Yes Sir."

"Tell the Lieutenant to make sure the night patrols march loudly through the town."

Ail smiled. "Yes Sir. Will do Prime Minister."

Commodore Ail passed the word down the chain of command to Lieutenant Yat who, after being sent more soldiers now commanded over two thousand soldiers. All traffic in and out of the small town was stopped. Anyone wanting out was sent back into town to let everyone know what they were facing. Anyone wanting to come into the town had a choice to make. They could continue to another town or camp there until the blockade was over.

By this time the Zim civilians were allowed to elect a mayor of their town that reported once a month to a Stylus governor that was over any given area. Each area called States had fifty to sixty towns in them.

The Governor of the State where Johm was, was named Getton. He was an overly kind governor that forgave many offenses against him and other Stylus there. This angered the Stylus under his command. However; after hearing what happened to the soldiers in his state he decided to come down on the citizens in the town.

Getton talked with Lieutenant Yat about not allowing any food or water into the town. The military now had full control over the town so the governor could not give the Lieutenant the order to do it. However; in this case the Lieutenant agreed with the governor. Lieutenant Yat was at least allowing food into the town but now even that stopped. In less than a week food was running short in the small mining town.

All of this was not bothering Johm. He and his disciples sat safely in the home of a man that built homes. The man had a wife and two young children. One day one of the man's children came up to Johm and sat beside him.

"Are you Muchee?" the young boy asked.

"No." Johm quickly advised him. "I am only a man spreading the teachings of Muchee.

"What teachings?" the boy asked.

"Blessed is the man that takes time to teach the youngest of these what Muchee teaches us all."

"Am I wrong in punishing my child?" the mother of the boy asked.

"No." Johm quickly said. "Sometimes a child must be punished but not to the extreme. If you spank your child then that is punishment but if you beat your child then that is abuse. The other men of the town should also beat you to show you what if feels like to be abused."

"How do I know when I have sinned?" the boy asked Johm.

"How can a boy that knows no sin ... possibly sin?" Johm advised. Then he looked at the boy and added; "As you grow you will learn these things but I say to you that if you do something that you know is wrong then that is a sin to you."

"How can you calmly call my son a sinner?" the mother asked.

"I am not calling your son a sinner woman." Johm insisted. "I am simply teaching him the things that you have not. I ask you woman. Why have you not taught your children these things?"

The woman looked down and said nothing. She knew that she was wrong.

"I say to all of you." Johm said. "The father is the leader of his family. As their leader he takes care of them and feeds them. He sees that they have a home and education for their future. But I tell you that he is also responsible for making sure that his family knows the teachings of Muchee. This responsibility lies on his shoulders alone. If a woman is alone with no husband but she has children then this responsibility falls on her."

As Johm continued to teach the family and a few of their friends the soldiers were searching homes for him. Finally the man that owned the home learned of the soldiers so he moved Johm and his disciples into an underground room. The man had built the underground room to store food for bad times. Now it hid Johm and his followers.

Later that day the soldiers knocked on the builder's door. He allowed them in to do their searching. A table with many things on it sat of the door that lead down to the underground room so no one would notice the loose door by walking on it. Four soldiers looked around while two others held rifles on the builder and his family.

Suddenly the boy yelled out; "Muchee teaches us to love each other. Why do you not love us?"

Before leaving the Sergeant walked over to the young boy and knelt in front of him. "You a good young man and you have earned my respect." Then he stood and walked to the door of the home. As he stopped he turned and looked at the boy again. "We will not harm your family."

Down in the underground room Johm heard all of this and was so proud of the boy. He knew then that he had reached the boy and hopefully his parents as well.

When the soldiers left Johm and the others came up to the den of the home. The soldiers had interrupted the meal that the wife was cooking but now it was time to eat.

The builder was not a wealthy man but he did have plenty for them all to eat. That was the reasoning behind the underground room; to store food. The room was always cool and perfect for keeping food safe. The builder also had a smoke house outside where he smoked meat. Once it was properly smoked the meat and some cheese was moved to the underground room where it kept for many months.

The soldiers continued to move from home to home searching for Johm. It took three days to search all of the buildings in and around town but they still found no Johm. Not sure what to do next Lieutenant Yat continued the blockade.

Then one of his men mentioned allowing people to exit the town but not go in. This might cause Johm to try to escape while carts and wagons can be easily searched. Yat decided to do it.

Over the next week many in the small town left for other towns with food. The Zim people were angry over the people of the town being starved into handing over Johm but the Lieutenant continued.

Back on Stylus Bubba knew what Lieutenant Yat was doing. The Zim had cost him a few friends and maybe one in his family. He no longer cared how the people of the small mining town felt. Johm was being hid by those people and he wanted his son back.

Meshet sat at her desk and looked over some of the reports coming in from around the galaxy. She had to read them and decide which ones to send to her father.

Suddenly Meshet stopped. It had been a few weeks since she had seen her brother's thoughts. "Dad." she said getting her father's attention. "I see Johm again."

"Tell me what you see." Bubba encouraged her.

"He is ... sitting in someone's home and talking to them. A little Boy ... either Stylus or Zim boy is sitting in his lap." Then she saw nothing else. "I'm sorry Dad."

"That's okay Baby Doll. We'll find him."

Chapter 8

Fill the Quarries

Johm was able to sneak out of the town during a storm at night. Although the soldiers that were making the circle around the town did their job well the blinding rain kept them from seeing four men walking past them and towards the mountains to the east. Once in the mountains the storm settled down and then stopped. Johm looked back at the town and the ring of soldiers around it. With a smile he turned and continued over the mountain.

Back on Stylus Bubba was having a hard time as Prime Minister. Not only were the gun activist hounding him but crime was still going up. Violence against Police had tripled in the past year leaving an average of three police officers being killed each week. The resistance movement rioted every weekend and most of the attacks on the police were by their members.

The constant reports coming in from the planet Zim saying that Johm had not been found also took it's toll on Bubba. The reports continued to show how that Johm was changing for the worst. He now saw himself as a Holy Man that was promising the Zim that he was a Prophecy Child. He promised the Zim that he would lead them back to being the powerful people they used to be. He had become a traitor to the Stylus people.

It was easy to see that Johm had been brainwashed. Meshet said many times that her brother was rebellious but this was taking it to the extreme. Now that Johm had moved to the planet Zim she was seeing his thoughts more often. She also noticed that what she was seeing was more powerful. At times she thought that she was able to send him her thoughts. But was he getting them?

From time to time Johm saw his sister's thoughts but

dismissed them as a daydream. Then one evening he realized that his sister really was reaching out to him. This meant that she probably knew where he was and this made it easier for him to be captured. He had to go into hiding again. Looking for a cave he hoped to block his sister's ability to see his thoughts.

Not having Johm around Stogy and Obi went back to Stylus where Stogy took control of the local resistance movement. He knew that the efforts of the movement had not accomplished much for a long time. This meant trying something else. Here was where Obi would come into the plan.

The movement started a rumor and quickly spread it around. The rumor was that after Johm left Stylus the Prime Minister met with Obi and started a love affair with her. Now she was pregnant with his child. The truth was that Obi was not even pregnant but, like on Earth, people believed the worst about someone. The truth did not matter.

Of course those in the palace knew that the rumor was nothing but a lie. Bubba seldom left the palace except to go home at the top of the hill. The resistance did a good job at making it look like the eighty-three years old Prime Minister was incapable of doing his job. Soon the citizens started to doubt his being able to do his job.

Seeing what was happening Yunnan and Bubba worked together to come up with a plan. Yunnan and Yushera were unable to have a child so that meant that when Yunnan died Bubba would become the King of Stylus. But now the people that once loved this human from Earth, no longer did.

Yunnan and Bubba finally decided to go on the attack. Orders were sent out to the military and police to capture any resistance movement leaders. The charge was trying to overthrow the Stylus government. Although she was not considered a leader of the movement the warrants were extended to Obi as well. It worked.

In just a few days many of the resistant movement leaders had been captured and the rumor was all but completely silenced. Among the captured were Stogy and Obi. Obi was tested and found to not be pregnant and this news was sent out to all newspapers in the area.

Judge Jester handled all of these cases except for Stogy and Obi. Bubba handled their cases. He had the courtroom filled with reporters to make sure that what happened got out to the people. The first to be brought into the courtroom was Obi.

Obi was scared. She knew that the crime of trying to overthrow the Prime Minister was an executional offence. She stood in front of the Prime Minister with a guard on each side of her. She said nothing until questioned by the Prime Minister.

"Your name is Obi ... right?" Bubba asked.

"Yes Sir." Obi said afraid to say to much.

"And you have spread the rumor around that I had an affair with you and got you pregnant."

"No Sir." Obi quickly insisted. "I didn't do that."

"I have witnesses here that will testify that you were with others yelling this rumor out for all to hear." Bubba informed her. "Should I call them up here?"

"It was a lie to make you look bad but I didn't start it." Obi replied.

"Then tell me who did." Bubba ordered her.

Obi thought for a moment. She knew that she was facing possible execution and life in prison was starting to look good. She had to convince the Prime Minister that she was only a pawn in this rumor.

"I ... am not ... sure." Obi said.

"Then I will give you some time to think it over so you can be sure."

Then he ordered that Obi be sent to the palace jail for an hour. As her guards walked her out of the courtroom and into the hallway she saw Stogy standing there with his own two guards. Looking back she saw him being taken into the courtroom. Suddenly she feared what Stogy might say.

Now Stogy stood in front of the Prime Minister like Obi had only moments earlier. He was afraid of what charges he was facing and had no idea what Obi had already said.

"So you're Stogy." Bubba said looking down at him.

"Yes Sir."

"You started this rumor about me having an affair with … the young lady that just left the courtroom and getting her pregnant."

"I never started that rumor." Stogy insisted.

"Then tell me who did." Bubba said.

Thinking that Obi had already fingered him Stogy said; "Obi did it." he insisted as he looked up at the Prime Minister. "It was all her idea."

"She said it was your idea." Bubba insisted. "Frankly I don't believe either of you."

"I was your son's friend." Stogy said as if he thought that it might help.

"Yes … that reminds me." Bubba said. "Where is my son?"

"The last I saw of him he was heading to Zim." Stogy replied. "I tried to stop him but he left anyway."

"He left where?" Bubba asked.

Stogy thought for a moment. He did not want any questions that might lead to his abducting Johm. "He left here … Stylus."

"I can call a Supership Commander in here that will say he saw you, Obi, and Johm on Prompt 4 so how could he have left here and gone to Zim?" Bubba asked with a hint of anger in his voice.

"You must be wrong Prime Minister." Stogy replied.

Bubba waved at a guard at the door. He stepped out in the hallway and brought in a young man. It was the man that escaped the shipyard with Obi and another girl.

"Does this man look familiar?" Bubba asked Stogy. Then he ordered Obi to be brought backing the courtroom.

"What is your name?" Bubba asked the young man.

"I'm Botcher." The man said.

"Now calm down Botcher." Bubba tried to ease the man's mind. "After your testimony you'll be going home."

"Don't tell him anything." Stogy yelled at Botcher as he

tried to break away from the security that held onto him. "You talk and I'll kill you."

Bubba looked at the security holding Stogy and asked them to take him out in the hall. When he was gone Bubba got back to Botcher.

"Now don't worry about him." Bubba assured Botcher. "He is facing a long time in prison if not worse but you are facing no charges. I only want to know a few things."

"Yes Sir." Botcher stated.

"Where do you know Stogy from?"

"I was in their gang." Butcher said.

Botcher went on to tell how that the gang went to the shipyard where Stogy and Johm were captured. He and the two girls, including Obi escaped. Then he told his Prime Minister how that he left the gang but heard that Stogy and Obi had put Johm in a shipping container and shipped him to Prompt 4. Later Johm must have gone to Zim.

Bubba sat there looking at Botcher. "You can go home now Botcher. And thanks for bringing me closer to my son."

"But I didn't Sir." Botcher said. "You already knew that he was on Zim."

"But you still confirmed what all happened ... things that I was not sure of." Bubba advised. "Now go over in the corner by the door and when Stogy is brought back in just leave behind him."

"Yes Sir." Botcher said as he turned and headed for the corner.

"And Botcher ... thanks again. Stay away from the gangs. You're a good man but if I see you in here because you are in trouble I will come down on you then."

"Yes Sir."

Bubba called for Stogy and Obi to be brought into the courtroom. As they were escorted in Botcher left without them seeing him.

"You two are ..." Bubba said but was interrupted.

"I don't care what you want." Stogy yelled as loud as he could.

86

"Gag him." Bubba ordered the security there. After Stogy was gagged Bubba continued. "You two are found guilty of many things including conspiracy to overthrow a Prime Minister and even kidnapping of my son." But you two will suffer two different fates."

Stogy still struggled with security so Bubba handled his case first. "I sentence you Stogy to life in prison with no chance of parole. And Obi ... I sentence you to ten years in prison with no chance of early parole."

Bubba ordered security to take them to two different prisons. As Stogy and Obi were taken away Bubba smiled. One of the security asked him why he was smiling when he still did not know where Johm was. He looked at the security officer and said; "But I just put away two of the people that helped turn my son against me."

The new leader to the Resistance Movement was Stumb and he was not among the captured resistance members. A warrant was issued for his arrest. Judge Jester gave all of the other captured resistance members five years hard labor in the rock quarry.

Control of Stylus was starting to come back to the government. The Resistance Movement was slowly being crushed. The public stated looking down on those that tried to make the Prime Minister look bad. Citizens were even starting to turn in their friends that were Resistance members. Safety while walking the streets at night was coming back.

Although things were looking better for Stylus Johm was still missing. Bubba knew that the people on Zim were hiding his son and they were starting to believe the lie about the Prophecy Child.

Meshet was having an especially hard time as she continued to see her brother's thoughts. Many times she would sit still and just look off into the distance as her brother's thoughts ran through her mind. And yet she could do nothing. None of his thoughts showed her exactly where he was. They all knew that Johm was on Zim but it was a large planet and the people were hiding him.

What no one on Stylus knew was that an old enemy had been in hiding but was getting ready to show themselves. The three children of Bok had been hiding on a far away planet. Baa, Maa, and Satie had been given their own Superships with a crew of thirty each. They landed their Superships on a small planet on the other side of the galaxy. Then they and their crews covered the ships with dead vegetation to hide them.

Each time a Stylus Supership flew by the planet they only got a faint metallic signature but nothing worth checking out. The three children of Bok and their crews lived in caves. There was no shortage of live game to eat and water to drink. This planet was the perfect hiding spot but now it was time to come out of hiding.

Baa, Maa, and Satie took one of the Superships and captured a cargo ship. After killing the crew they took the cargo ship to the planet they had the other two Superships on. The planet's name was Sop 2. Using the cargo ship the three and a few of their crew went to Zim to find out what was going on. To their amazement Zim was under Stylus control but the people were being allowed to move around. Then they heard of Johm; an old enemy. However; this time he just might be an ally. They had to meet with Johm to find out.

Johm was doing some serious hiding. He never stayed in one place for more than two nights. He now had six disciples but that number constantly changed. His disciples did not have to hide because they were not wanted. Now that the Zim knew who Johm was, finding a place to hid for a day or so was no problem.

One night Johm spoke to the people of a small area when he was approached by two male and one female Zim. For a short time Baa, Maa, and Satie spoke to Johm asking him questions.

"Are you just a religious leader or the leader of the Zim people?" Baa asked.

"I am both." Johm said. "I teach the teachings of Muchee but I am also the Prophecy Child. I am here to lead the people of Zim to freedom from the Stylus."

"But the prophecy is of Prophecy Twins not one child."
Satie said.

"That is what the Stylus want you to believe." Johm
explained as everyone around listened. But I am Zim so how
can I lead the Stylus. They already have control over this
planet. They do not need anyone to lead them to freedom. They
already have their freedom."

"But aren't you the son of the Prime Minister of Stylus?"

"For many years I thought that I was but I was a child that
he kidnapped and took in as his son. I was kidnapped from a
hybrid family here on Zim."

Baa, Maa, and Satie looked at each other and then at
Johm. "Could we speak to you in private?" Baa asked Johm.

Of course." Johm agreed. "Let's go into the home I will be
sleeping in tonight."

Once in the home the four gathered in a back room to talk.
The wife of the home brought them all food and drink. Then
the three introduced themselves to Johm.

"Yes … I know you … the children of Bok." Johm shocked
them.

"How do you know who we are?" Maa asked.

"I know more than you think I know." Johm advised. "You
are the ones that I have been waiting on."

"Why were you waiting for us?" Maa asked."

"I need to build an army and you have a small army that
needs a leader." Johm explained.

"How do you know this?" Baa asked.

"You are Baa aren't you … the older son of Bok who the
Prime Minister of Stylus killed?" Johm asked.

Baa, Maa, and Satie looked at each other. Then Baa said;
"I am and you are the Prophecy Child." Baa replied. "How
may we serve you?"

The three children of Bok continued to talk with Johm
until late in the night. But one thing still stood in their way.
They only had three Superships against the sixty-five warships
and seventy-five Superships that Stylus still had.

The next day Johm went back to Sop 2 with the three

children of Bok so he could teach them what he wanted. His disciples spread out as far as they could and started building a fighting force against the Stylus.

Weapons building machinery was taken apart and put on cargo ships. When the Stylus army asked what they were doing the Zim said that the machinery was being melted down. The Stylus military believed the story. The truth was that the machinery and workers were being taken back to Sop 2 and put back together. Before long weapons were being built again.

Johm spent the next four months teaching the words of Muchee and telling them what he wanted in not only freeing those on Zim but destroying Stylus. "We will not only crush the people of Stylus but we will crush their spirits."

While Johm was on Sop 2 the Prime Minister of Stylus thought that Johm was still on the planet Zim. Thousands of Stylus soldiers were looking for Johm and thought that they had him pinned down a few times. But they only found out that he must have slipped by them yet again and again.

Report after report cane over Meshet's desk for her to choose which ones went to her father, the Prime Minister. But with all of the reports saying that Johm had only escaped by them she passed none of them to her father.

More and more often Johm was starting to see his sister's thoughts. They started as just flashes in his mind but he finally started seeing more. That was when he realized that she was probably seeing his thoughts as well. Not knowing what to do about this he just continued to teach the crewmembers of the three Superships.

"He's teaching a group of people." Meshet told her mom and dad as they sat at a dinner table in the palace lunchroom. "I can't tell what he is teaching them but he is still teaching them something."

"Can you see where he is?" Bubba asked.

"I can only see that he is in a room ... but that's all." Suddenly Meshet gasped for air and sat backing her chair as if in shock.

"What's wrong?" Becka asked her daughter.

90

"He just looked over his left shoulder and … right at me." Meshet insisted.

"Then he knew that you were listening to his thoughts." Bubba explained.

"He even smiled as if he knew he … just now scared me." Meshet added.

These short looks into her brother's life was starting to get to Meshet. Every now and then she was caught sitting alone and crying. Meshet loved her brother and tried over and over to let him know that over the many light years of space. But his thoughts seemed to become more and more evil. Now he seemed to look over his shoulder and right at her with the intent to scare her. Meshet knew that she was loosing her brother.

Bubba and Becka began to worry for their daughter. Rommin and Coman also worried for their sister. They were so angry that they wanted to go looking for Johm just to hurt him in a serious way. Everyone thought that they were just mouthing off but they were serious.

Finally Rommin and Coman talked to their father about going out and searching for Johm on their own. "But you sent out spies so why not us?" Coman asked.

"Because you are not trained spies and you have jobs here." Bubba insisted.

"Rommin looked at his brother. "I think we need to take a vacation don't you?"

"Oh yes." Coman agreed. "I am so tired and we have never had a vacation."

"Okay boys." Bubba said. "Cut it out."

"I have a second in command for things like this." Rommin said. "This would give me a chance to see how he can do in charge."

"I think Dad can do without any public relations for a while." Coman added.

"Okay!" Bubba agreed. "You two can take a vacation but … we will organize this … vacation."

Chapter 9

DNA

Rommin and Coman got permission from their father to take a long disserved vacation. The truth was that they would look for their brother Johm. Bubba used this and asked Meshet to send messages to Johm that Rommin and Coman were looking for him. He hoped that Johm might come and meet them.

Johm's disciples had formed three very large armies to move on Johm's orders. The plans to attack the Stylus soldiers on Zim was set but they waited for Johm's orders to move. Weapons came into Zim from Sop 2 marked as food. Everything was set and everyone waited on Johm's word to attack.

However; everything stopped when Johm saw his sister's thoughts about Rommin and Coman looking for him. An overwhelming urge to see his brothers stopped Johm and his plans.

As Johm paid attention to his sisters thought he learned that Rommin and Coman were heading to Zim. Not wanting them to get hurt he put the attack on hold. Then he took the cargo ship to Zim to meet with his brothers.

When Rommin and Coman left Stylus they had everything that they needed in order to survive but, they required very little. When they arrived on Zim the military already knew that they were coming and had things set up for them. Being the sons of the Prime Minister they had more security than they really needed. Lieutenant Yat was there to meet the two brothers when they arrived.

"Welcome to Zim." Lieutenant Yat said as Rommin and Coman got off of the cargo ship. Yat had about forty of his soldiers with him. "I will not be able to be with you all of the time but these soldiers are your security."

"You expecting a war Lieutenant?" Rommin asked about the forty member security team. "Isn't this a little excessive?"

"I just don't want you two to get hurt while you're here." Yat explained.

"But we are hoping to find our brother." Coman said. "He isn't going to come to us if he sees even one soldier around."

"That's true." Yat admitted. "So how can I see to your safety while you are here?" Yat asked.

"You don't." Rommin insisted. "Our father wants us to find Johm so please keep your security away from us."

"Of course." Yat agreed. Then he showed the two where they would be sleeping. After they got settled in Yat showed them where they could eat. The military compound was a safe place for them but they would not be fallowed if they left the compound. They would be on their own.

Rommin and Coman rested that day and night. But the next day they left the compound to look for their brother, Johm. The word quickly got around the people of Zim that Johm's two brothers were looking for him. On the third day they got their wish.

Two Zim men approached Rommin and Coman and asked them a few questions.

"We hear that you two are looking for Johm." one of the men said.

"We are his brothers." Rommin said. "Do you know where he is?"

"We'll ask the questions and then we'll decide if we should take you to him." the other man said rudely.

Of course." Rommin agreed.

"Why do you want to see Johm?"

"Because he is our brother and we have not seen him in quite a while." Coman told the man. "We love our brother."

Before we agree to take you to him you will need to loose the two spies fallowing you."

"What spies?" Rommin asked.

"The two in black shirts." one of the men said as he

pointed at the two he spoke about.

Coman might have been the younger of the two but he was stronger. He walked over to the two men wearing black shirts. ""You two falling my brother and me?"

"No Sir." one of the men insisted.

"If I see you two behind us again I'll come back and make sure that you two have a serious accident." Coman said. "Do we have an agreement gentlemen?"

"Yeah sure." they both said.

Coman walked back to his brother and the other two men. "I asked them not to fallow us." he told his brother.

"And if they still fallow us?" Rommin asked.

"Then they will have a serious accident." Coman advised. "Let's walk and see if they do fallow."

The four men walked around for a while and continued to look back. The two that had been fallowing Rommin and Coman were not see again. Then suddenly Rommin and Coman were pulled into a doorway. The door was shut behind them. As they turned they saw Johm standing in front of them. The three men hugged and then sat down. Food and drink was brought to them as they talked.

"So what have you two been up to?" Johm asked his brothers.

"Just looking for you." Rommin said. "What the hell are you doing?"

"I am doing what Muchee has instructed me to do." Johm replied.

"You're full of ... crap Johm." Coman spoke his mind. "You're acting crazy."

Johm remained calm. "I'm fulfilling the prophecy of the Prophecy Child."

"That's Prophecy Twins you stupid idiot." Coman was getting mad.

"Calm down Coman." Rommin advised. Rommin was more diplomatic.

"Why should I?" Coman asked.

"Because I am the elder brother and I need you to calm

94

down some." Rommin advised.

Coman looked down at the flood. "Yes brother."

"He has respect for you." Johm told Rommin. "That is good."

"I am the elder of the three of us." Rommin advised Johm.

"Yes you are but ... if you're going to tell me to come home ... don't waste your time. I answer to Muchee not you."

"We believe in Muchee as well but Muchee would not tell you to go to war with your own people." Rommin advised.

"But I am the Prophecy Child." Johm insisted.

"You're one of two Prophecy Twins." Rommin said.

"Oh yes." Johm said. "How are Lesst and Meshet anyway?"

"Doing a lot of crying because of you." Coman yelled out as loud as he could.

"Coman." Rommin uttered wanting his brother to keep his voice down some. Then he turned his attention to Johm. "Your sister Meshet spends a lot of time crying over you."

"She isn't my sister." Johm advised. ' "You stupid fool." Coman said before shutting up again.

"Coman is right." Rommin said. "You are a stupid fool. She is not only your sister but your twin sister."

During the battles with the people of Zim I was grabbed from a hybrid family on Zim and then given to your father ... the Prime Minister. He raised me as his son and told everyone that I was Meshet's twin. This was done to fulfill the prophecy of the Prophecy Twins which he made up.

Rommin looked at Johm as if he was crazy. "Who warped your mind to think that?"

"Who warped your mind into the lies you believe?" Johm asked.

"Well ... a simple DNA test can tell us exactly who you are." Coman calmly advised. "Unless of course your to much of coward to take the test."

"Oh isn't he so cute ... trying to call me a coward." Johm said.

Coman quickly stood while Johm slowly stood. Then as

Coman started to step towards Johm, Johm slowly waved his hand. An invisible force slid Coman a few feet to his left.

"How did you do that?" Coman asked.

"I just seem to have some abilities that others do not have." Johm explained.

"What else can you do?" Coman asked.

Johm smiled. "Well my brothers ... I need to go."

"Why do you call us your brothers but Meshet is not your sister?" Rommin asked. "She is the main reason why we are here."

"Well ... you are my stepbrothers and she is my stepsister but that is all." Johm tried to convince them.

"No Johm." Rommin said. "We may be your stepbrothers but Meshet is your twin sister and if you had any balls ... and evidently you don't ... you would take that DNA test."

"I don't need any test to tell me who I am ... or in Meshet's case who I am not."

"I guess he is a coward." Coman told Rommin. "Just like you said he would be."

Johm smiled. "You're not going to get me to give in to your wishes." Johm insisted.

"But that's all it could be." Rommin said. "You're afraid of finding out that Meshet really is your twin sister."

"I'll tell you what." Johm said. "If you can bring that test here then I'll take it."

"We can take a blood sample right now and take it back to compare it to Meshet's blood as well as Mom and Dad's blood." Rommin said.

"The reason he gave into the test was probably because he knew that we did not have Meshet's and Mom and Dad's blood samples with us." Coman said.

"Okay then." Johm said. "Take your sample from me and take it back home. Then you'll know."

"And just how would we get the results of the test back to you?" Coman asked.

"I don't know." Johm said. "Maybe come back to Zim and let me know you're here?"

"It would be easier if we could just call you somehow." Coman suggested.

"Yes but then the military would also be able to find and grab me too." John said. "Now I need to go. Just come back with proof that I cannot denounce and let it be known that you are here. Then I will find you like I did this time."

"We love you Johm." Rommin advised. "We are not giving up on you."

"Do as you wish but you two must be off of this planet before tomorrow morning." Johm said.

"We can't leave until midmorning." Coman told him.

Johm thought for a moment and then said; "Okay then ... by noon be off of this planet."

"We will but what is happening at noon?" Rommin asked.

"Just don't be here." Johm advised. "I don't want you two harmed."

Johm allowed Rommin to take a blood sample from him and then asked his brothers to leave. As soon as Rommin and Coman walked out the front door Johm was rushed out the back door. Within minutes Johm was hustled out of the town.

Rommin and Coman went back to their room in the military compound and rested the rest of the night. The next morning they talked with Lieutenant Yat about what Johm had said. The Lieutenant laughed at the idea that there could be any type of uprising from the Zim. He refused to believe that it could happen.

After being laughed at Rommin and Coman took another cargo ship back to Stylus. As the cargo ship flew away from the planet Zim they got a warning. The planet of Zim was under attack.

Three large groups of armed Zim attacked and took over the military compound and town around it where Rommin and Coman had been only minutes earlier. Other smaller Zim forces cleared the area around the town. Just under two thousand Stylus soldiers had been captured with another one thousand reported dead.

The three Superships of Baa, Maa, and Satie attacked the

97

five Stylus Superships patrolling the Zim airspace. The sudden and unexpected attack caught the Stylus ships off guard and all five were destroyed with three of them crashing into the planet.

Then a warning was sent to Stylus Command telling them to keep their Superships away from Zim. If they refused then the three Superships would attack them. Normally this would have been no problem but the Zim advised Stylus Command that Johm was on board one of their Superships. They could not attack without taking a chance of killing the Prime Minister's son.

By time reports came in about the attack and the three Zim Superships Bubba had already gone to his office. It was in the early morning on Stylus still three hours before sunrise. Because of what had happened Meshet was also there.

"I'm to old for this." Bubba said to anyone listening. "I am really getting tired of this boy." he added about Johm.

"What are you going to do Dad?" Meshet asked.

"I don't know." Bubba said. "I can't keep pampering Johm."

"I hate saying this Dad but ... you're gon'a have to kill him. He's gone to far now."

"What do you see?" Bubba asked Meshet. "What is he thinking right now?"

"I can't just make it happen Dad." Meshet advised. "It just comes to me from time to time."

"So ... nothing is coming to you." Bubba uttered.

"No Dad." Meshet said. "Not right now."

Bubba sat back in his high back chair and thought. As he was deep in thought Yunnan walked into Bubba's office. Sitting in the chair in front of Bubba's desk Yunnan looked at his Prime Minister.

"I know you love your son but sooner of later you will have to do something." Yunnan advised.

"Yes Sir ... I know." Bubba replied and then took in a deep breath. Letting out a heavy sigh he stood. "I going to order the attack on the three Zim Superships."

"Dad!" Meshet yelled as she stood. "Johm is on one of those ships."

"I know Baby Doll." Bubba said. Then he looked at her and added; "If you can do it ... let your brother know that he is about to die."

Bubba left his office and went to the Comm Room. From there he contacted Commodore Ail and ordered the destruction of the three Zim Superships around the planet Zim. Then he contacted Commodore Zu and ordered all of the transport ships to be filled with his soldiers and sent to Zim. Once there they would regain control of the planet Zim. Now it was a matter of waiting the two days it took the ships to get from Stylus to Zim.

The next day the cargo ship that Rommin and Coman were on arrived at Stylus Command. They wasted no time taking Johm's blood sample to the palace medical room. DNA from Bubba, Becka, and Meshet were already there. Within minutes the information was there for all to see. Johm was the child of the Prime Minister and his wife Becka and Meshet was his twin sister. Now; with another war being fought on Zim, how would they find Johm again to show him?

The day after Rommin and Coman got back to Stylus fifty Stylus Superships attacked the three Zim Superships and the planet Zim itself. Johm was not on any of the Zim Superships. When he was rushed out the back door after meeting his brothers he was taken back to the cargo ship. Then he was taken back to Sop 2.

One and a half million Stylus soldiers reinvaded the planet Zim and forced the armed fighters into surrendering. Any Zim caught with a firearm was executed on sight. This time the soldiers were more harsh against the Zim people than the first time they took the planet. Fathers and mothers found to be holding firearms were executed right in front of their children. Kindness was shown to any children left with no parents. They were taken to an area where they were given food, water, and medical care.

Once the one and a half million Stylus soldiers were on the

planet Zim Commodore Ail called back all of the Superships except for one squadron. This squadron was commanded by Commander Revis of the Second Squadron. He was a hybrid married to Lesst, one of Bubba's two daughters.

No one knew that Johm had not been killed when the three Zim Superships were destroyed until Meshet saw his thoughts again. "He's alive." she said to her father. "Johm is alive."

"You see him?" Bubba asked.

"Yes Sir." Meshet said as she stared straight ahead. "He's walking on a dirt road. But that's all I can see."

"It's okay." Bubba assured her.

While the people of Zim suffered for backing Johm on a false prophecy he was safe on Sop 2. Vegetation covered the cargo ship and the crew of five, not to mention Johm himself, got ready for another long stay. With enough food and water to supply over eighty crew members of the three Zim Superships for over a year they were set for a long time.

Bubba was not taking it well about ordering the death of Johm. However; he also knew that he had no choice. The Zim uprising had to be stopped and there was no time to talk to Johm anymore. In fact Johm was the cause of the uprising. He saw himself as the prophesied savior of the Zim people.

Bubba and Becka did not know if they should have a funeral for their son Johm. Meshet said that she saw his thoughts but she was not sure. Then Meshet got a report from one of the Stylus spies on Zim. Johm was seen escaping Zim in a cargo ship just before the attack on the Stylus military compound.

"I told you he was still alive." Meshet happily admitted.

Bubba and the others were happy to learn that Johm was still alive. But now Rommin and Coman wanted to go back and find their brother again. This time they would be armed with DNA proof that Johm was the son of Bubba and Becka and the twin brother of Meshet. Not knowing where Johm went to Bubba cleared Rommin and Coman's trip back to Zim.

Three days later Rommin and Coman headed back to Zim. The military compound was a safe area again with over four million Stylus soldiers in and around it. When Rommin and Coman got back to Zim they were rushed to their room. Terrorism had become the tools of war for the Zim.

In the effort to use Zim sympathizers as security they accidentally got a few Zim that used it for their own agendas. This always happens. A government takes over an area of country and the enemy is trusted to a point to help. This is stupid as it never works. About five to ten percent of those that want to help their people use the idea and turn against the conquering foe. They almost always wait until they are armed and then use those weapons against their enemy. How stupid do you have to be to want to arm an enemy thinking that he will help you work against his own people?

The Zim were not only doing this but they would earn the trust of the Stylus soldiers and then walk among them with bombs strapped around their bodies. Setting off the bombs they carried would many times kill fifty or more Stylus soldiers. This was a tactic that Bubba had seen used by terrorist groups on Earth but never before with the Zim. But Bubba knew how to fight this.

Anyone on Zim found to be wearing bombs around their bodies was killed on the spot before they could use them. However; because of this new order only one or two might have surrendered only to be executed anyway.

Chapter 10

The King of Stylus

Suffering a major defeat the people of Zim turned against the prophecy of the Prophecy Child. After all; how could they believe in a prophecy that no one had even heard of until recently. They knew that Johm had lead them into this hardship. Being defeated once was one things but a second time made it even harder to except. However; Bubba understood this.

Rommin reported back to his father about how the people of Zim felt towards Johm. The people of Zim were now crushed physically and morally. There were still many of them that continued to fight the Stylus soldiers but for the most part the people of Zim submitted to the ruling Stylus. It was easier to submit than to fight a fight that they could not win anyway.

By time Bubba finished reading Rommin's report on the people of Zim he felt for them. He then sent out an order to be easy on the people of Zim. Work with them as long as they did not fight. Come down harshly on those still fighting but be merciful to those that needed mercy.

One day Bubba asked Yunnan about making Governor Puut Governor of Zim. "We need someone there to be in charge of the entire planet." Bubba suggested. "Having the military in charge is only making public relations worse."

Yunnan thought for a moment. "He would be good there." Yunnan agreed.

"Then should I ask him to do it?" Bubba asked Yunnan.

"Yes." Yunnan agreed. "Please do it but now I need a replacement for him."

Bubba went back into his office and called Governor Puut to come to his office. That evening Puut got the word and came to see his Prime Minister.

"Good evening Prime Minister." Puut said as he walked into Bubba's office.

Bubba stood and met Puut in front of his desk. After shaking hands both sat in their chairs.

"Have you ever considered moving up in politics?" Bubba asked Puut.

"Not after my wife died last year." Puut said.

"That's right." Bubba remembered. "I forgot about that. How have you been doing?"

"Pretty good I guess." Puut said. "I'm still waiting to go another hunting trip though."

"Those were the days." Bubba admitted with a big smile. "But I did call you in here for another reason."

"And what is that Sir?" Puut asked.

"I talked to the King and we would like to move you up to Governor of the planet Zim." Bubba said calmly.

Puut sat there looking straight ahead. For a while he was unable to move. Then he looked at the Prime Minister and smiled.

"You want me to be the Governor of the planet Zim?"

"Yes we do." Bubba assured him. "You have done a great job here on Stylus for many years and now we want you to govern Zim. Do you except the job?"

"Oh yes Prime Minister." Puut said. "I have nothing nor anyone keeping me here."

"Good." Bubba said as he shook Puut's hand. "You need to take care of any affairs here and get there as quickly as you can. A large home just outside the military compound is being cleaned and repaired right now for you. Security walls are being built around the home and security has already been set up there for you."

The two men stood and shook hands again. Then Governor Puut left Bubba's office to take care of things so he could go to Zim. He was looking forward to this job.

Bubba walked over to Yunnan's office and found him not there. Security there told Bubba that Yunnan had to go to the medical room so Bubba walked down to there. When Bubba walked into the Medical Room he saw Yunnan laying on a gurney asleep. A nurse walked up to Bubba with her finger to her lips. Then she pulled Bubba out into the hallway.

"The King is not doing well this morning." the nurse told Bubba.

"What's wrong?"

"He's just old and still working hard." she told her Prime Minister. "Forgive me for saying this Sir but … maybe you should get ready to become King."

"Is he that close to death?" Bubba asked.

"If he does not stop working so hard." the doctor said as he walked up. "If the King does not stop … being King then he will die soon. Either way you will become our new King."

Bubba looked down. "I never really thought that this day would ever come."

"I have already warned the King and then gave him a sedative to help him sleep." the doctor said. "He is resting now."

"I need to talk to him as soon as he wakes up." Bubba mentioned as he turned and left Medical.

Once in his office he advised Meshet to let their family know about the King and that he might be appointed as King. The information was not to go beyond the family. She sadly agreed to do it.

About an hour later Bubba was called back into Medical. The King was awake. As he walked into Medical he found Yushera standing beside Yunnan holding his hands. When she moved Yunnan could see Bubba standing at the door.

"Come closer my friend." Yunnan told Bubba. Yunnan let go of Yushera's hands and reached out for Bubba's hand. As he held Bubba's hand he spoke.

"It looks like my days as King are over." Yunnan said. "Yushera and I have no children so you need to get ready to become the King of Stylus."

"But I am human not Stylus." Bubba insisted.

"You are a Stylus citizen and next in line to be the King of Stylus." Yunnan exerted himself saying. Then he lay back and struggled with his next few breaths. "I must do this or die soon. Therefore I appoint you as King of the planet Stylus."

"But Sir..." Bubba said but noticed that Yunnan had fallen asleep. The doctor checked Yunnan.

"He is asleep again ... my King."

Bubba took a few heavy breaths and then looked at the doctor. "Hearing that is not easy." Then he gave Yushera a hug and left Medical.

Upon returning to his office Bubba told Meshet that he was now King of Stylus. He asked her to pass the word around to everyone but let them also know that Yunnan was still alive but very ill. Then he had Meshet inform Rommin that he was now the new Prime Minister. Coman took his place as Head of Prisons.

Many in the military expected some type of big change but Bubba changed nothing. He lived by the saying; *Why fix what is not broken.*

The next day Rommin and Coman got the word of their father becoming the new King of Stylus. They also learned about their new jobs as well. Rommin was trying to get used to being called Prime Minister, something he really did not expect to happen. Johm should have become the next Prime Minister but he was busy fighting against his father.

Rommin and Coman stood in the military compound looking out the main gate. With some fighting still going on how would they find their brother? The people of Zim were now angry with Johm for leading them into another failed fight for freedom. They were not hiding him anymore. The people of Zim no longer embraced the prophecy of the Prophecy Child. Because the prophecy of the Prophecy Twins was for the Stylus they did not embrace it either. The people of Zim had lost all hopes until they started hearing things that the new King of Stylus had for them.

A few days later Rommin got a message from Meshet saying that she saw Johm's thoughts again. He was not on Zim. That changed his and Coman's mission. But they still did not know which planet Johm was on. Rommin decided that he had to get back to Stylus but Coman would stay there on Zim to find out where Johm had gone to. For the first time in his life Coman was alone.

Rommin learned that a Supership had been sent to Zim to bring him back to Stylus. As Prime Minister he would no longer travel on cargo ships. By time he got to the palace his father had already moved his things into the King's office. Meshet remained her father's secretary and had also moved her things into his office. Now her desk was at the door to the office. Anyone wishing to see the King had to see her first.

Rommin used his father's old desk. He needed a secretary so he asked his wife, Tesh. She excepted the job. With the family totally in control of the planet the people seemed to be happy. There were those few that were not happy no matter what happened but most of the people of Stylus supported Bubba and Rommin.

With Becka now being called the Queen she never really had any authority. If something happened to Bubba then Rommin would move up as King. She still had come a long ways from being just another hybrid on a Stylus warship to the wife of the Prime Minister of Stylus. Now she was the Queen of Stylus.

While Rommin was setting up his new office as Prime Minister Coman was still on Zim trying to find out where Johm had gone to. There was no need to leave the safety of the military compound so he stayed there.

One day Coman got word that an old woman wanted to see him about Johm but she would not go to the military compound. This meant that he would have to go to her. This was dangerous as she also asked that he come alone. He could not bring any security with him.

The next morning Coman left the compound. He showed his papers to the gate guards and was cleared to pass. He searched for a young man wearing a red shirt. Unfortunately; that morning every man in town seemed to be wearing some type of red shirt. Coman walked along the streets hoping to find the young man when finally he felt a tug on his shirt sleeve.

Coman stopped and looked down at a little hybrid boy of about six years of age.

"Are you the brother of Johm?' the boy asked Coman.

"Yes I am." Coman answered. "But I was looking for a young man not a young boy."

You should know that we hybrids do not like being called a boy." the young boy said. "The Zim used to call us boys all of the time. Now it is considered a word insulting us."

"My father told me of humans on Earth. The blacks were called boys even though they were sometimes old men. Now they are not called boys for the same reason."

"Thank you Sir. Fallow me."

Coman fallowed the young man to a home where he opened the door. Inside were a few older men and women, all hybrids. Then an old woman asked Coman to sit.

"You are the brother of Johm?" the old woman asked.

"Yes Ma'am." Coman replied. "My name is Coman."

"We hear that you are looking for your brother." an old man mentioned. "He is not here."

"I know that." Coman said. "I only know that he left for another planet but I don't know which one."

"Johm is not our friend so why should we help his brother to find him?" the woman asked."

"My brother believes that he is a Prophecy Child." Coman informed everyone there. "He does not believe that he is my father's son. I have DNA proof that he is my father's son but I need to show him. Then maybe I can get him to come home to Stylus."

"Those in the room whispered among themselves. Then the old woman said; "We will help you so that you might take this demon home with you. He has hurt our people badly. We do not want any more war and that is what he has brought to us. Now we are treated worse than ever by your father."

"My father is now the King of Stylus and he wants to stop the fighting among our people. He said that we are brothers and sisters. He wants us to live in peace but there are still many

Zim that want to fight us."

"Your father wants peace?" another old man asked.

"He is tired of this fighting." Coman assured them all. "He may be from Earth but he knows that the Stylus came from Zim almost one thousand years ago. The Stylus and Zim are brothers and sisters. Family should not be fighting."

"Wise words from someone so young." the old woman said.

"These are not my words but the words of the King of Stylus." Coman advised. "Let the fighting stop here ... now ... today."

Those in the room whispered again. Then the old woman said; "We think that your brother went to a planet named Sop 2. That is all we know and we are not sure of that."

"That's enough." Coman assured them. "I will try to find my brother and take him home with me. I thank you for your time."

Coman stood and the others there also stood. He shook their hands and thanked them again. Then he left and returned to the military compound. As he walked the boy walked with him. When they reached the compound gate they stopped.

"I like you ... brother of Johm." the boy said. "Please help us."

Coman went to his knees and gave the boy a hug. "I promise that I will do all I can to help your people." Then he stood and walked into the compound.

Coman wasted no time researching the planet Sop 2. As he sat at the computer an explosion was heard outside in the compound. A cargo ship had been shot down by a rocket fired from outside the compound. Immediately Stylus Superships destroyed the area where the rocket was fired from.

Unfortunately; the cargo ship that was shot down carried the new Governor of Zim; Governor Puut. He and everyone with him was killed. Coman sent word back to his father to let him know what had happened. Bubba thought for a moment and asked Coman to be a temporary Governor of Zim. He excepted.

After talking to Commander Zub who now commanded three thousand Stylus soldiers on Zim he went to the newly rebuilt Governor's Palace. Security was very high with over one hundred soldiers assigned as palace security. About thirty worked actual security with another seventy soldiers on call to respond in less than one minutes if needed.

Once Coman got settled in he went to his office and sat in the big high back leather chair. He remembered what he had promised the young hybrid boy. *I promise that I will do all I can to help your people.* Of course he did not mean only the hybrids of Zim but the Zim themselves. He broke out some paper and a pin and started writing down changes that he wanted to make. The young boy's name was Runin so he called what he wrote The Runin Act.

In the Runin Act he called for an end of all of the fighting. Anyone found with a firearm was given no less than ten years in prison. Anyone that shot a Stylus soldier would face execution. There were many animals on Zim but for the time being hunting was not allowed with no one being allowed to own a firearm. Under the Runin Act he promised that as soon as the fighting stopped hunting with firearms would be allowed again. The Runin Act had many more parts promising more freedom as soon as the fighting stopped.

Coman had farming tool brought in so that the people could grow their own food. Large herds of Bocka were brought in for other Zim to raise and sell to feed the public. By time the first three months had gone by the people of Zim were living as they did before the war started. Under Governor Coman they were happy again.

But in every civilization there are those that wake up in the morning with only one purpose in life. They are the trash of any civilized society. They are the criminals that rape, kill, and destroy. They are the drug dealers and low lives in a town. They want nothing more than to destroy the perfect harmony of all that live there. They do not want to be a part of any good will.

With that in mind Coman formed a local police

109

department. This idea spread to all of the towns in the area. Jails and prisons were built and filled with the criminals that committed crimes against others. Within six months of Coman becoming Governor of Zim crime was all but eradicated.

But through all of this Johm was still not found. A search from space of Sop 2 turned up nothing about Johm. Johm knew that he could not go back to Zim with so many hating him now. He blamed this hatred of him on his father; the King of Stylus. He could not believe that he mislead anyone. The failed rebellion on Zim had to have been because of unseen problems that popped up during the fighting. Now with the Zim people hating him he could not go back to Zim. He struggled with the story of the Prophecy Child.

How could he now lead the people of Zim out of the hands of the Stylus if they hated him. Life on Zim was getting better and this did not help him either. Somehow he had to convince the people of Zim that they may seem to be living better but they were still living under the iron fist of the Stylus. Finding a way to do this would take time.

Bubba and the others in the palace still worried about Johm. Finding him was impossible. Bubba did not want to move into the palace as long as Yunnan was still alive. He was doing better but was still weak most of the time. Yushera and a medical team took care of him.

Bubba let Coman run Zim the way he thought was best. He was doing a great job anyway. By time the sixth month of Coman's being Governor of Zim Bubba asked him to take the job permanently. Again Coman excepted.

Everything on Stylus was going well also. Although the people of Stylus loved Yunnan they also loved Bubba. It did not matter to them that a human from Earth was their King. When Yunnan was feeling better a date was set for Bubba's inauguration. Bubba was already the King but the inauguration just made it official.

The inauguration ceremony started with Bubba standing at the front door to the palace. Yunnan sat behind the King's desk in the King's office. Then Bubba slowly walked "The

Walk" to the King's desk. This was required. Then Yunnan stood behind his desk and shook Bubba's hand. After handing the gavel to Bubba Yunnan stepped around to the front of the desk as Bubba stepped behind it. When Bubba sat in the chair behind the desk he was officially the new King. After that everyone there reached over the desk and shook the new King's hand. This signified that they excepted him as the new King.

Bubba stepped out from behind the desk where Becka joined him. Coman and Johm were the only ones in the family that were not there. After a few minutes of more hand shaking everyone moved into the ballroom except for Bubba and Becka. After everyone was seated at their tables Bubba and Becka came into the ballroom. As they walked down the middle of the ballroom everyone stood and clapped their hands. The clapping continued until Bubba and Becka were on the platform and seated behind the table facing everyone else. Also at this table was the King's family.

As usual there was more food than could possibly be eaten in one sitting. There was the usual roasted ova, ova sausage, and many other dishes with meat and vegetables in them. Although this was a night of happiness it was also a night of sorrow.

Towards the end of the night Yunnan collapsed. The excitement was to much for him. He was carried to a table and laid on it where he passed away. Needless to say the celebration was over. Most everyone left while some of the higher ranking military officers saw the former leader to the hospital where Yunnan was legally pronounced dead.

Becka stayed with Yushera through the night where neither one of them got any sleep. Bubba stayed at the hospital until the autopsy was finished. Yunnan had died from a massive heart attack. The doctor said that Yunnan died instantly. There was no pain.

Chapter 11

Johm's New Connection

Johm learned about his brother Coman becoming the new Governor of Zim and that the people of Zim were living better under his rule. He wanted to talk with Coman but could not go to Zim. So he sent word by messenger hoping that his brother might meet him someplace safe for them both.

By this time Johm had moved again. This time he hid on a small and long forgotten planet called Noter 3. The workers that were stripping the crashed warships that had crashed on the planet had left long ago. With all of the scrap medal left behind no Stylus Supership would ever notice the small cargo ship there. Johm and four followers lived in the barracks that had been built for the workers. He sent one of these followers to contact Coman.

A young Zim named Joshen went to the planet Zim to contact Governor Coman. As he arrived he was asked why he came back. He simply told the Stylus soldier that he had heard that conditions were better there and he wanted to come home. The soldier believed him.

Joshen stopped by the Governor's gate and asked to see the Governor. Of course the soldiers laughed but when he mentioned Johm's name they stopped laughing. Another soldier was called to the gate which lead Joshen into the Governor's home where he sat for almost an hour before being called.

Joshen was taken into a large office where the Governor sat behind a large desk. For a few minutes he stood in front of the desk. Finally Governor Coman looked up at him.

"You have word from my brother Johm?" Coman asked.

"Yes Sir." Joshen said. "He wishes to meet with you but he cannot come to this planet. He wishes to meet someplace where you both will be safe."

"And how would I get word to him of any meeting place?" Coman asked.

"You would tell me and I would take this information back to him."

"I will allow you to spend the night in my home." Coman said. "Tonight we will eat and discuss this meeting. Is this expectable to you?"

"You would have me stay in your home tonight?"

"Of course but you would be under guard until you leave tomorrow morning." Coman said. "Meeting my brother is important to me and I need you to take something back to him."

Joshen was taken to a room where he cleaned up and changed into clean clothes provided by the Governor. Later that evening he was called to dinner with the Governor.

Joshen was lead by two guards to the dining room of the Governor's home. It was a small room built for feeding only a few people. Most of the time the Governor ate in this room. Joshen sat down in a chair across the table from Governor Coman. Food and drink was brought out for them and they ate as they talked. It was finally agreed that Johm would meet Coman on an island on the other side of Zim. It was a desolate place but secure. Coman said that he would have security there for his protection but promised that his brother would also be safe.

After eating the two men shook hands and went to their own rooms. The next morning Joshen went back to his cargo ship and left Zim airspace. He took a long rout back to Noter 3 in case he was being fallowed but the Governor kept his word. The cargo ship was not fallowed.

When Joshen gave the news to Johm he then left to continue his duties. Johm looked at he DNA report and thought about it. But he had been so brainwashed that he threw the report into the fire and dismissed it as a fake report. It had to have been doctored up to look real. He thought about the meeting and decided to do it. The meeting would take place one week later.

Johm sent Joshen back to Zim and to the area where the meeting would be held. His job was to keep an eye open for any traps. Johm trusted Coman but he had no idea what the Stylus military might do. The Governor had no control over the military. However; Coman did talk with Commander Zub and asked for his cooperation. The Commander agreed to not try to capture Johm during this meeting.

The day finally came and Governor Coman took a transport to the island where he was to meet his brother. It was a nice day. A table had been set up in a clearing with only two chairs, one on each side. A small campfire was started and a pot of water boiled for making coffee hung on a hook and chain above it. Coman even had milk and sugar for the coffee. This was also symbolic. This way Coman could invite his brother into the camp to talk. Johm excepting a cup of the coffee meant that he would show no aggression.

Finally a cargo ship hovered a short distance from the camp. Then it moved closer and landed at the other end of the clearing. When the door opened on the cargo ship Johm stood in the doorway. After looking around he stepped off of the cargo ship and walked up to his brother.

Coman handed his brother a coffee cup and then filled it. After pouring his own cup they went to the milk and sugar and doctored their coffee. Then they sat down to talk. Only then did they speak.

"It's good to see you again my brother." Coman said with a smile.

"Good to see you too." Johm said. "However; I am confused with the DNA results you sent me through Joshen."

Coman smiled. "I like Joshen. He is very respectful."

"Yes." Johm replied. "He is a very good young man but ... back to the DNA test."

"It's true Johm." Coman told his brother. "You are the son of our father and Meshet is your twin sister."

"I think you doctored up the results of the test." Johm insisted.

114

"You and Meshet read each other's minds all the time." Coman reminded his brother. "Only twins can do that."

"I can read the minds of others." Johm insisted.

"Oh really." Coman argued. "Then what am I thinking right now?"

"I can't just read minds. Your thoughts have to come to me."

"Above all things be true to yourself." Coman said. "If you were really a Holy Man then you would know that and yet you lie to yourself anyway."

"I am sorry Coman but I do not believe this test."

"You're a fool Johm." Coman argued. "You have been brainwashed into this stupid way of thinking."

"My teacher would have never lied to me Coman."

"Do you remember being taken from Stylus?" Coman asked.

"I don't remember much about that day." Johm said trying to remember.

"What do you remember first?"

Johm thought for a moment. "I remember … Obi and Stogy hiding me from Stylus soldiers. One time they almost found me."

"What else?' Coman asked.

"I was taken to a cave where my teacher trained me in the ways of Muchee."

"And just how does Muchee teach you ways of war?" Coman asked. Muchee is the son of God and he does not teach war."

"Stop." Johm insisted. "I'm getting a headache."

"Okay Johm." Coman said. "I don't want to hurt you but the DNA test is true."

Without any warning Johm stood and walked over to the open door of the cargo ship. He stopped long enough for a split second to look back at Coman. Then he stepped in the cargo ship and the door closed. Seconds later the cargo ship lifted off and flew into space.

Coman stood there looking up into the sky. He still had no

idea as to what to expect next. *Did Johm believe the DNA*? He was not sure. He climbed into his transport and flew back to the Governor's home. Then he sent a message back to his father.

> Met with Johm. He has the
> DNA results but still does not
> believe it. I do not know where he
> went when he left.

When Bubba got the message from Coman he got depressed again. They were so close and yet still did not get Johm. One day Coman got word from his Judge that a hybrid male came through his court telling how that he used to follow Johm. His name was Routen. Routen was convicted of taking food from a stand in the streets and was given one month in the local jail. Coman went to the jail to talk to the man.

Routen was brought out of his cellblock and taken to a room where he was chained to a chair. Across the table was a man wearing a hood so that his face could not be seen. When Coman looked up Routen recognized him immediately.

"Is that you Governor?" Routen asked.

"Yes it is." Coman said. "I hear that you were running with my brother Johm."

"Oh that was before the last war." Routen advised. "He left just before the fighting started leaving me and a few others here. Now we are trying to just survive."

"But I have almost taken care of all unemployment." Coman said. "You still unemployed?"

"Yes Sir." Routen said. "The people know us and that we ran with Johm. Now no one will hire us because of that."

Coman thought for a moment and then said; "If you tell me all that you know about Johm ... whether it helps or not ... I will get you a job when you get out of here."

"Why would you do that?" Routen asked.

"Because I need to find Johm and ... you need a job if you're going to stay out of trouble." Coman assured him.

"What do you need to know Sir?"

For the next hour Routen and Coman talked. Routen did not know enough to be of any help to Coman but the Governor kept his word. Come to find out Routen loved to cook so when he got out of jail in about two weeks he would start working in the Governor's kitchen. The present cook needed help so Routen would be doing that.

Nothing that Routen said was of any help to Coman. Routen did not know where Johm went to or where he might be at that time.

Johm was looking for another place to hide. Earth only had one Supership patrolling it's airspace now. Johm and the other four hybrid men flew to the opposite side of Earth than where the Stylus Supership was. The cargo ship flew into some woods close to Washington DC and hid. Looking human Johm left the cargo ship and made his way into Washington DC. His hope was to contact the new American President and try to make a deal with him.

Johm walked up to the main gate to the White House and looked in. His hair was long and shaggy and his clothes looked like nothing that anyone else would wear. He waited as he tried to figure out how to get to the president. Then finally he saw his chance.

Three black vehicles came to the gate as the President started to leave the White House. The crowd was moved back away from the driveway. As the second car started to drive out the gate Johm jumped in front of the car. The driver hit the breaks and Secret Service people jumped out of the first and last car with guns drawn.

They yelled for Johm to hit the ground but with a wave of his hand an unseen force pushed them aside. Then he looked at the Secret Service man on the ground close to him.

"I mean no one any harm but I must speak to the President."

By this time the other Secret Service had already surrounded Johm. They started to step in closer but someone ordered them to stop. The President saw Johm wave his hand

and push his Secret Service to the side. He knew that Johm had to not be human.

"Wait a minute." the President said from the door of his car. "Who are you?"

"My name is Johm but I mean you no harm Mister President." Johm answered. "A past President fought my father many years ago but my father destroyed the White House. I see you have rebuilt."

The president whispered to his driver and then looked at Johm. "Get in one of the other cars and do what the Secret Service tells you to do. Then they will bring you to me."

The President got back into his car. His driver pulled out on the street and turned around. Then he drove to the back of the new White House. Johm got into one of the other cars and it drove to the back of the White house as well. He was not allowed to leave the car until the President was safe inside.

When Johm got out of the car he was surrounded by the Secret Service. With one of the Secret Service on each side holding his arm he was lead into the back door of the White House. Once inside a force pushed the hands off of him.

"You don't need to hold my arms." Johm insisted. "Just lead the way in which you want me to go."

The Secret Service looked at each other and then did as he suggested. Johm was searched for any weapons and then lead to the Oval Office. Once in the office a line of Secret Service stood between Johm and the President's desk.

"Okay now just who are you?" the President asked.

"I am Johm. The King of the planet Stylus is now trying to kill me so I ask you for sanctuary."

"Why should I help you?"

"And your name is ..." Johm asked.

"I ask the questions here." the President snapped at Johm.

"Then that is okay." Johm said. "I'll just go to Russia and ask their help."

Not wanting Johm to go to Russia the President said; "My name is Marks. I am President Michael Marks of these United States."

"Thank you Sir." Johm said trying to be polite. "Many years ago the Prime Minister of Stylus attacked your country and destroyed your White house. He is now the King of Stylus. I'm sure you remember that."

"And so ... again ... why should I help you?" Marks asked.

"Because I can help you to dominate the airspace around this planet and the planet itself."

Marks sat back in his chair. He liked what Johm was saying. They continued to talk for a while as Johm told Marks how he could help. The President was the first Socialist elected as President of the United States. After being in office for one year he and already abolished Congress and the Senate. The original Constitution was taking out of it's protective case and burned. Freedom was nonexistent.

Bread cost $6.00 a loaf and crime quadrupled during the first year of his being President. Welfare was bankrupted in less than a year with money going to anyone that chose not to work because they just did not want to. The nation was all but destroyed which had been the goal of the Liberals in the country for many years. The southern border wall that a Republican President had rebuilt was bulldozed down again and illegal aliens crossed into the United States by the millions each year.

Not willing to admit that it was his Socialist ideas that destroyed the country the President looked for a way out. Now Johm was offering that way out. The President even gave a bedroom to Johm and allowed him to stay in the White House. Marks had all but become a full dictator so he saw the White House as his home. Elections were abolished and anyone that was in a political office just stayed there.

Over the next few days Johm convinced the President to allow him to have Superships built. However; there was still one Stylus Supership in orbit that would stop them. The Supership watched the Black Sands area of New Mexico but not the thick woods of the Mountains in North Carolina.

The United States were already building two Superships in

119

the North Carolina mountains. They were using designs from some of the Superships that crashed many years earlier. Marks planned to use his Superships to shoot down the Stylus Supership that was patrolling Earth's airspace. Then he would use them to take over the world.

The government had been working on rebuilding the two Superships for many years. Two months after Johm go there the Superships were finished. The crews trained on them while still on the ground. But finally they had to lift off and test other parts of the ships. They did this a few times without the Stylus Supership seeing them. Then one day they lifted off and met the Stylus ship in space.

Without any warning the two Earth Superships attacked the single Stylus Supership. Within seconds the Stylus ship was burning in space. The two Earth ships transported as many of the Stylus off of their ship as possible before explosions on board started. They took nine Stylus prisoners. Twenty-one died.

The prisoners were taken to a federal prison where security was high. American soldiers were added to the security in the cellblock where the Stylus prisoners were kept.

The next day the Stylus Supership finally hit Earth's atmosphere and started to burn up. A few hours later it crashed into the Pacific Ocean about half way between Hawaii and Guam. That is where the seven mile deep Mariana's Trench was located. Retrieving the crashed ship would be impossible even for another Supership.

Now knowing how to build the Superships the President wasted no time in supplying all of the money needed to build them. He used political prisoners as slave labor to build more Superships. During this time Johm helped the President to develop communications to contact Stylus. Johm insisted that Stylus was not to know that he was there.

When Marks finally contacted Stylus Command he asked to speak for the King. All of this was done with information and instructions from Johm.

"Tell us what you want and we will get the information to

the King." Stylus Command ordered Earth's President.

"No!" Marks said. "We have nine prisoners from your Supership. If I am not talking to your president in fifteen minutes then I will execute one of them every fifteen minutes until I am talking to him."

It was quiet for a few minutes as it took time for the messages to travel over such a distance. Then the words came over the radio. "We're getting the King."

Bubba was awaken and told what was going on. He quickly got dressed and ran to the Com Room. Earth's communications was patched through to the palace Comm Room.

This is the King of Stylus." Bubba said. "Who am I speaking to?"

Although communications had improved greatly over the years it still took ten minutes to get an answer back from Earth.

"This is the President of the United States. We have captured your crew of the Supership that used to patrol our skies. Unless you want them executed stay away from our airspace. We do have two Superships patrolling our airspace so keep away."

"Could we talk to you about making a deal. If you will return our people to us we will agree to stay away from Earth. It's not like you are a threat with only two ships."

"No trade." the President said. "Just stay away and they will remain safe."

"May I send someone to check on these prisoners you have and talk with you farther?" Bubba asked.

Marks thought for a moment. This might give him an opportunity to get more weapons. If he could gt better weapons then he would be able to control the whole planet with no problems.

"I agree with this but let me know when someone is coming." Marks said. "Otherwise they may get shot down. Letting me know will assure their safety.

"Agreed." Bubba said. "I will let you know before someone

is sent."

Bubba called Rommin into his office. He told Rommin what went on and said that he would be the one going to Earth. Rommin would leave the next day.

Chapter 12

Meeting Another President

Rommin got ready to go to Earth and meet with the President of the United States. His wife Tesh did not want him to go.

"I don't trust this president." Tesh insisted. "He is not one of the good presidents on this country."

"I know Honey Bun but it is my job as Prime Minister." Rommin told her.

After hugging the kids and Tesh one more time Rommin went outside to a transport. The transport took him to Stylus Command where a Supership waited for him. Four other Superships waited in space for him to come to them. Commander Mat now commanded all five Superships.

Rommin went to his room as the Supership lifted off and flew into space. Then all five Superships flew off towards Earth. Later Rommin was in the lunchroom when Commander Mat walked in.

"There you are Prime Minister." Mat said as he got a glass of water. "May I join you Sir?"

"Of course Commander." Rommin replied.

"May I ask what your mission is?" Mat asked his Prime Minister.

"It's no secret." Rommin said. "I am going to Earth to talk to the President of the United States. He is holding some of the crew of the Supership they shot down."

"I haven't heard of this." Mat said. "What happened?"

"It seems that this President has used some of the crashed Superships from when my father attacked them and rebuilt two of them. Then they went into space and surprised the Supership that we had in Earth's airspace and shot it down. Now they control Earth's airspace."

"Like I said … I have not heard this."

"The King kept it quiet but the story can get out now."

"I would like to let the other ship Commanders know if you don't mind." Mat mentioned.

"No problem here." Rommin admitted.

Mat got up and went straight to Communications on the Bridge. From there he sent out a message to the fleet telling them what happened. When Commodore Ail got the message he was angry with Mat for not informing him first. But when Rommin told Ail that he cleared Commander Mat to pass the information on Commander Mat was no longer in any trouble. Mat still got a serous butt chewing on using proper protocols.

It still took three days to reach Earth. One day before arriving Rommin sent a message to the American President letting his know that they were only one day away. In order to keep any fighting from starting Rommin had the four escort Superships hold far out in space. The Supership he was on would go in alone.

Commander Mat did not like holding the escort ships so far away but he also understood. Their five Superships would have made easy work on the two Earth Superships but it would also put the mission in danger not to mention the life of the Prime Minister and the lives of the captured crewmen.

Unknown to Rommin Commander Mat had already talked to Commodore Ail and twenty Superships were also sent. They were only a half a day behind the four escort Superships. While Rommin was on Earth talking to the American President the twenty Superships met with the four escort ships and waited with them. They were far enough away from Earth that they could not be detected.

Rommin transported right into the Oval Office of the White House. As he stood in front of the President's desk he was searched for any weapons. Only after being cleared the President walked into the office. Walking around Rommin he stared. Then he sat in his chair behind the desk.

"Please sit." Marks said.

Rommin sat in the chair to his left. "I would like to see…"

he said before being interrupted.

"I don't care what you want." Marks yelled out. "You're in my office now."

"I did some research on you before getting here." Rommin said with a smile.

"And what did you find out?" a very arrogant Marks asked.

"You are the worst President that this nation has ever had right behind that other one that my father calls President Obomination. You have totally destroyed this nation in less than two years and now you are hoping to get something from me to help you take over and destroy the rest of this world … right?"

Marks was angry. "I can have you thrown into a prison where your King would never find you if I wanted."

Rommin brought up his wrist and spoke into the communications device. "Commander Mat. Are you ready to destroy this country?"

"Yes Sir. Just waiting for you to not call me every fifteen minutes." This had already been set up before Rommin transported to the Whitehouse. "And one more thing Mister Prime Minister. Another twenty Superships have arrived under the orders of Commodore Ail."

Rommin was upset with Commodore Ail sending the twenty extra Superships but it did not show in his face. He had to make it look like it was just part of his plan.

"And if I do not report every fifteen minutes this country of yours will be utterly destroyed starting with your precious White House … again." Rommin advise the President with a big smile.

"You think you're smart don't you?" Marks asked.

"Oh … I'm a lot smarter than you are my favorite little dictator." Rommin insulted Marks as he continued to smile.

For a few seconds Marks just stared at Rommin. "What is it that you even want?"

"Well like I started to say earlier I need to see the prisoners."

"You can't see them." Marks insisted. "They are locked up far from here."

"Then how can I report back to my King that they are safe?" Rommin asked.

Then a voice from behind a curtain said; "Oh they are safe my brother." Johm stepped out from behind the curtain and walked over to Rommin.

Rommin jumped up to hug Johm. "What are you doing here?"

"Just trying to hide with your father trying to kill me and all."

"Now you know that's a lie but you're good at lying." Rommin said.

"Now all of these insults are going to help neither of us today." Johm advised.

Rommin thought for a moment. "You're right. I'm sorry."

"That's okay my brother."

"So you two are brothers?" Marks asked.

"Actually half brothers." Rommin said.

"No … actually no brothers. I was kidnapped from a Zim family and raised by his father as his son." Johm said.

"And we showed you the DNA results." Rommin reminded him. "Stop being stupid Johm."

"There you go with the insults again." Johm said. "Your heart is full of anger and your mind is full of hate for me. You want me dead as well don't you?"

"Look into my mind Johm and you will see that, that is not true."

Johm was quiet for a moment. Then he said; "I see nothing."

"Again I ask what you're doing here today." Marks reminded them.

Rommin looked at Johm and said; "I need to see the prisoners."

"Let him see them." Johm told Marks.

"I don't fallow your orders." Marks yelled as he laughed.

Johm looked at Marks and held up his hand. Instantly

Marks grabbed his face as blood started pouring out of his nostrils. When Johm lowered his hand the bleeding slowed to a stop.

"You will fallow my orders from now on and I don't have to be anyplace around you to start the bleeding again." Johm informed him.

One of the Secret Service ran into the office with two rolls of paper towels to mop up all of the blood on the President's desk. The President sat down in his chair as others helped him to stop the bleeding.

"That should shut him up for a while." Johm said. "I need to go now Rommin. I am sorry but I do not believe that I am the King's son."

"You had the DNA results. Just think about it."

Suddenly Johm looked straight ahead as if he was in a short trance. Then he looked at Rommin. "Meshet is still trying to find me."

"And how could she see your thoughts if you two were not twins?" Rommin asked. "It happens all of the time with hybrids."

"I don't know but ... I need to go." Johm said as he turned and walked out of the Oval Office.

Rommin tried to fallow Johm but the Secret Service stopped him. Right then he got a call from Commander Mat. "You okay Sir?"

"I'm okay Commander. Keep checking every fifteen minutes and if I do not answer you then you know what to do." Rommin spoke into the communicator on his wrist.

"Yes Sir." Mat answered.

"Now Mister President ... could I see the prisoners?" Rommin asked.

Not knowing that Rommin could not do the things that Johm could do Marks waved his hand to one of the Secret Service. "Show him the prisoners." he said with his noise pointing up with a paper towel still holding back the blood.

"The prison where they are at is a few hour's flight from here." the Secret Service said.

"Well I'll tell you what." Rommin said. "I'll fallow your plane in my ship and then transport down to you when we get there."

The Secret Service officer thought for a moment and then said; "Yes Sir."

Rommin called Commander Mat and within seconds transported back up to his Supership.

"How did it go Sir?" Mat asked.

"Pretty good." he said. Then he lowered his eyebrows and added; "I think."

When the Secret Service plane landed on a tiny airstrip the Supership hovered cloaked. Then it uncloaked but engaged the shields in case someone with an itchy finger started shooting. Rommin transported down to the surface. Two cars came out of the tunnel and picked up the Secret Service and Rommin and took them inside. The Supership used it's sensors and watched them through all of the rock and metal walls until they stopped where the prisoners were being held.

Rommin talked with the prisoners in Stylunese so that the Secret Service and guards would not know what was being said. Rommin told the prisoners to be still and wait. He still needed to talk to the American President.

When Rommin and the Secret Service were back outside he transported back to the Supership and left for the White House. The Supership was cloaked so the public had no idea that they were even there. Once back to the White House Rommin transported into the Oval Office again.

"Back already?" Marks asked.

"Yes Mister President." Rommin said. "I came back leaving your Secret Service and their slow plane behind. I hope you don't mind."

"No no." Marks said. "I have more of them than I can shake a stick at."

Trying to appear to be nice Rommin asked; "How is your nose Sir?"

"Oh it stopped bleeding as soon as you left." Marks said thinking that Rommin kept it bleeding until he left.

"That's good." Rommin replied. "Now we need to talk about getting our crew back but ... I do want to thank you for taking good care of them. Two were wounded and your people took care of them as well. Thank you Sir."

"Well you're not getting them back." Marks insisted.

"May I ask why not?"

"Because your crew were patrolling our sanctioned air space." Marks said. "That was an act of war."

"Well in a way ..." Rommin said with a smile that irritated Marks. "We were at war many years ago."

"You're not getting them back." Marks insisted again. "And if you keep hounding me about it then you will be joining them."

"Just to make sure that I know where I stand ... you are threatening me?" Rommin asked calmly.

"Let's just call it a serious warning." Marks said with his own smile.

At that time two Secret Service grabbed Rommin and took the communicator off of his wrist. "Now lets see you call for help." Marks said.

"I don't need to." Rommin calmly said. "If I do not report backing about five minutes your Washington DC will be leveled." Then he smiled again and added; "And our weapons can now reach you all the way down in your bunker."

Marks got mad and ordered the Secret Service to let Rommin go. "Give that thing back to him too."

"Thank you Sir but I really must go now." Rommin said as he pushed a button on his communicator that instantly transported him back up to the Supership. Once he was back on board he had Commander Mat fly back to where the prisoners were being held. Once there he had the prisoners relocated and then transported up to the Supership.

Rommin had the other Superships capture the two Earth Superships if they could but that was not about to happen. The two Earth ships fought but they were to overwhelmed. In less than a minute they were both burning in space. Only fourteen of the two crews were transported to a Stylus Supership as

129

prisoners.

With the crew of the downed Supership on board Commander Mat moved the Supership back to the White House. Rommin had Mat uncloak the ship but put up the shields. If they were fired on even by rockets they would not be harmed. The reason for uncloaking was so that the public would see it. Rommin hoped that old memories would come back to the people and that this might cause the American President problems.

Rommin walked over to the Comm Center and had the person there turn on the outside speaker. He wanted everyone to hear what he was about to say.

"Mister President. This is Rommin; Prime Minister of the planet Stylus. We have our kidnapped crewmen back. The next time we catch you building any Superships we will level Washington DC. Maybe millions will die and I ... don't really care. I have only known you for a few hours and I have had enough of you." Then Rommin thought that he might put an idea in the minds of the public. "Maybe your people should rise up and overthrow you. We will be back to see how you are doing and I will be leaving many of our own Superships behind to make sure you do not build anymore Superships."

Rommin spoke to Commander Pilk who commanded the other twenty Superships and asked him to keep five Superships there to patrol Earth and watch the American ground for any Supership building sites. Pilk left a Commander Kopi in charge of the five Superships that would stay.

Rommin and the remaining Superships returned to Stylus. He sent a message back to the King telling him what all happened and that he was bringing back the captured crew of the downed Stylus Supership. The King was happy.

When Rommin and the others got back to Stylus the people of Stylus were happy. They were very pleased with their new Prime Minister. At first many worried about a hybrid being their Prime Minister but they thought the same thing about Bubba. Bubba proved himself and so did Rommin.

About a week later the planet of Stylus had a celebration

for the freed crewmen welcoming them back home. They were treated as heroes. The celebrations around the planet lasted for two days.

During the celebration the crewmen were brought to the palace where they were given medals for heroism. Their conduct as prisoners was considered exemplary. That night the palace threw a ball for the crewmen. In a solemn ceremony before eating the names of those that died that day were read off.

After eating everyone in the ballroom mingled. This was the first chance that the rescued crewmen were able to shake Prime Minister Rommin's hand. They were so thankful.

The next day Bubba and Rommin were so tired that they took the day off of work. Security at the palace enjoyed the quiet. But with them being relaxed a man was allowed to walk into the palace unchecked. Just inside the door of the palace he was challenged by security. At this time he pulled a string that set off a bomb that he was wearing. There was little damage to the palace but a great deal of blood and body parts had to be cleaned up. Two of the palace security were killed and another one was injured.

Because of this Bubba and Rommin got to work. Bubba and Becka lived upstairs of the palace in the King's Chambers. Yushera now lived in a large room beside them. Rommin, Tesh, and their children now lived in the home at the top of the hill behind the palace.

After the explosion Bubba came downstairs. He stopped where there was blood and part of an arm. As he looked around he saw sprayed red on the white walls and blue floor. Security had a path cleaned so that the King could get to his office. Becka and Yushera came down the stairs but went back to their bedrooms when they saw all of the blood and body parts.

Bubba ordered that the fingerprints be taken from one of the hands so that they might know who it was that carried out such a cowardly crime. Someone was going to pay for this. When Rommin finally waded his way into the King's Office they talked about the attack on the palace.

That evening Rommin got the report on the fingerprints taken from the bomber. The fingerprints belonged to a known members of the Resistance. Now the Resistance was escalation their crimes. Now murder seemed to be their goal. As Rommin left to go to his office Bubba broke out some paper and a pen. As he wrote he condemned the actions of the group and made it a Felony to even be a member of the Resistance. From then on anyone found to even be a member of the Resistance faced no less than twenty-five years in prison. Any Resistance member that harmed a police officer faced the death penalty. Just harming a citizen might case someone to face the death penalty also. This attack on the palace was the last straw. The King was putting up with the Resistance anymore.

Shortly after signing this into law the local police captured a hybrid that was the leader of the local Resistance. His name was Stumb. Stumb had a long record of crimes against the citizens and government of Stylus. He was arrested after a warrant was served on him. He was presently wanted for attacking a local police officer. Bubba wanted to handle this case himself.

Bubba talked with Judge Jester and asked that Stumb's case be sent to him. Jester had no problem with it. It was very unusual for the King to judge over anyone but Bubba wanted to ask him a few questions. Finally the day came and Bubba sat in the judge's seat in the palace courtroom. Stumb had to be brought from the regular courthouse just outside the palace gate. When he saw that he was being brought to the palace he knew that he was in some serious trouble.

"Your name is Stumb … right?" Bubba asked knowing that it was his name.

"Yeah!" Stumb said showing no respect to the king.

"You beat up one of my local police officers and left him for dead." Bubba looked down at the man. "How do you plea?"

"Not guilty." Stumb said smiling in defiance. "I didn't do a thing."

Bubba looked at one of the jailors and asked; "How is the officer doing."

The jailor stepped forward and said; "The officer that was hurt is my friend Sir. He knew this man and called him by name when he was questioned. He was attacked three weeks ago and is still in the hospital."

"Why is he still in the hospital?" Bubba asked.

"As this man attacked him he stabbed the officer three times. Two of those stabs punctured one lung."

"Will he be okay?"

"Yes Sir but he was hurt bad."

"Thank you for your testimony." Bubba told the jailor. Then he turned his attention to Stumb. "What is your story?"

"He was messing with me and I didn't like it." Stumb said.

"How was he messing with you?" Bubba asked.

"He wanted to search me for weapons only because he thought that I was part of the Resistance."

"Well are you?"

"No I'm not." Stumb said.

Bubba thumbed through some papers on his desk. "I see here that you have been arrested many times for crimes related to the Resistance."

"I can't help that." Stumb said smiling.

"Well I'll tell you what I believe." the King said. "I believe that you are the leader of the local Resistance and being the leader I feel that you planned or at least helped in the planning the attack on the Palace."

"No. That's not true." Stumb was starting to get scared.

"Do you know someone named Obi?"

"I know no one with that name." Stumb said.

"How about Stogy?"

"Don't know him either." Stumb insisted.

"Well they both know you and they admitted that you took over the Resistance after Stogy went to prison."

"That's not true." Stumb pleaded.

"And one more thing Mister Stumb." Bubba said. "I know you myself. You attacked one of my daughters about a year ago. She was not hurt bad but you did hurt and robbed her."

"I didn't do it." Stumb yelled.

Bubba waved his hand at the guard at the door of the courtroom. He opened the door and in stepped Meshet.

"Meshet." Bubba said. Make sure your right but ... is this the man that attacked you about a year ago?"

Meshet looked closely at the man. "Yes Sir." she said. "I remember the scare on his left cheek."

"Thank you Meshet. You may go if you wish."

"I would rather stay and see what he gets for what he did."

"You may but please sit down." Bubba told her. Then he turned his attention back to Stumb. "Mister Stumb. I find you guilty of trying to kill the police officer in question and for the attack on the woman that just identified you. Because of your record I deem you a danger to the public and sentence you to death."

Stumb started yelling so Bubba had him gagged. Then he continued. "You will be taken to the prison where tomorrow morning you will be hung in view of the public. Let everyone know what will happen to members of the Resistance from now on.

Stumb was taken away and the next morning was hung in plane view of the public. Now everyone knew the fate of leaders of the Resistance and what would happen to their members that hurt a police officer.

Chapter 13

Johm

There was an uproar from a small part of the public that complained about everything the King did. All he had to do was exhale and they would complain. Bubba called them Liberals because they were just like the Liberal Communist of the United States on Earth. All the Liberal Communist on Earth wanted was things that would destroy the country. Now with a Socialist in the White House, President Marks personally saw to the destruction of America. The Liberals on Stylus were trying to destroy that planet for many years before Marks was elected.

It took three days to clean up the palace. By time they finished the smell of rotting flesh and blood was starting to get bad. It would take another week of bleach and hot water to get the smell out of the walls.

Bubba now knew that Johm was on Earth and probably living in the White House. The five Superships that Rommin left to patrol Earth would keep him there. No interplanetary travel to or from Earth was allowed. Without any Superships Earth did not have the capabilities of interplanetary travel anyway.

Coman was starting to get a taste of his own Liberals on Zim. Although the people of Zim had the freedom to say what they wanted there was a small group that constantly complained about everything Coman did or even said. They were never happy about anything. But because most of the population was finally doing well the Liberals of Zim stayed a small group.

Bubba did not worry about Johm anymore. Unable to leave Earth he would not be able to cause anymore problems. What no one knew was that Johm had the plans to build land based particle cannons. These cannons could fire at ships in space. The American President had already started building these cannons all around the United States just after Johm got there. The cannons were simple to build so within five months thirty two had been built.

One day Marks and Johm wanted to test one of the particle cannons. They had three of the cannons target one of the Stylus Superships. All three cannons fired one round at the same time. These particle cannons fired particles of Gremite which traveled at light speed. It was like firing a large shotgun with the pellets traveling at light speed. When the Gremite particles hit the Supership they totally destroyed the Supership. The Gremite particles traveled right through the ship causing it to instantly loose it's atmosphere. One second the crew was breathing and the next second there was no air. The crew died instantly as if they had been shot into space.

The other four Superships hovered on the opposite side of Earth so that they would not meet the same fate as the other Supership. Commander Kopi instantly notified Stylus Command about what happened. When the word got to the King he was furious. He knew that Johm had something to do with this. Earth had no particle cannons so Johm had to have done it. What bothered Bubba was what else Johm might have told the American President.

Bubba went to the Comm Room and sent a message to Commodore Ail. He ordered the Commodore to have Commander Kopi fire on any ship trying to leave Earth and destroy it.

"But Prime Minister." Ail said. "Your son could be on that ship."

Bubba thought for a moment. The next words were hard to say but he had to. "You have your orders Commodore."

"Yes Sir." Commodore Ail said. "I'll inform Commander Kopi right now."

"Thank you Commodore." Bubba said.

Bubba turned and saw Meshet standing in the Comm Room doorway.

"You just ordered the death of your own son?" she asked. Flames of anger shown in her eyes. "Then maybe I will join him so you can order my death as well."

Meshet stormed out of the palace. Bubba thought that she might be going home to pack a bag and go to a place in the forest that she loved to go to when she wanted to be alone. What he did not know was that she meant what she said.

Meshet went to Stylus Command and told them that she was on a secret mission and needed a ride to Earth. There was a small cargo ship doing nothing so she took it. A three man crew with two pilots lifted off the surface and headed towards Earth. This small cargo ship was not very fast so it took four days to reach Earth.

While Meshet was on her way to Earth Bubba still thought that she was at her hiding place in the forest. Wondering when she might come back to work he did the best he could without her.

"She must have been mad." Rommin said as he walked into the King's office. "Do you know where in the forest she goes to?"

"No idea at all." Bubba said.

"She'll be back soon enough."

"I hope so." Bubba replied. "Her paperwork's piling up."

By this time Meshet had contacted Commander Kopi and told him that she needed to meet with him. When her cargo ship reached him she transported to Kopi's ship.

"So how is the King doing?" Kopi asked Meshet.

"He is okay." Meshet said. "He sent me on this mission hoping that Johm might listen to me."

"I'll need to contact Johm and make sure that they do not fire on you. Ma'am." Kopi said. "Those particles canons would rip your tiny cargo ship apart."

Kopi and Meshet walked to the Comm Center where he contacted the American President.

"Johm's sister is here and wants to meet with Johm." Kopi told Marks.

"Stand by and let me see if he wants to meet with her."

Marks said.

Then Marks sent someone to get Johm. About fifteen minutes later Johm walked into the Oval Office. He asked Marks what was going on and then learned that Meshet was already in Earth's airspace. He got on the radio and called back to Commander Kopi.

"Meshet is there with you?" Johm asked. Suddenly he felt something ripping at his heart.

"Yes I am Johm." Meshet said over the radio. "Now could I transport down to you without any worries?"

"Yes!" Johm quickly said. "Of course you can."

When Meshet appeared in the Oval Office Meshet and Johm grabbed each other and hugged for a long time.

"Why don't you two get a room." Marks said but he was not joking around.

"She is my sister." Johm told Marks.

"So you admit it." Meshet mentioned.

"My teacher, Stylum told me that I was kidnapped from a hybrid family on Zim and then raised on Stylus as the King's son."

"But you just admitted that I was your sister and I am his daughter." Meshet said. "However; I am here to be with you because Dad has ordered your death."

"He did it again?" Johm asked.

"He is tired of so many Stylus dying because of you." Meshet advised Johm. "Now you have told this bastard dictator how to make the particle cannons. You killed a crew of thirty on the Supership."

"I'm not a bastard little girl." Marks said.

"Calm down Marks." Johm advised.

Marks waved at two of the Secret Service and said; "If he raises his hand and my nose starts bleeding again … kill him. Then kill his sister."

Marks had Johm and Meshet taken back to his room. Unknown to them he had their water drugged. A few minutes later both Johm and Meshet were out cold on the floor. Johm was put on his bed and kept drugged and under control.

138

Meshet was taken to another room in the White House and laid on that bed. She was also kept drugged. Later the House doctor injected them with something that put them into a coma. They were constantly monitored to keep them safe.

Marks then contacted Commander Kopi and told him that he could destroy the White House if he wanted but he would be killing his Prime Minister's children. When the Commander reported back to the King Bubba was madder than he ever had been. Finding out that Meshet was on Earth took him by surprise.

Bubba calmly walked to the Comm Room where he contacted Commodore Ail. He gave very direct orders. There was no doubt as to exactly what the King wanted. "Totally destroy Washington DC of Earth but do not touch the White House. Also destroy any and all land based particle cannons."

Commodore Ail passed the orders on to Commander Kopi who commanded five Superships. They hid on the opposite side of Earth than where the land based particle cannons were. This new order could get them all killed. In order to complete this mission quickly and then get out of the area Kopi used all five ships.

Commander Kopi had all five Superships cloaked before they went into view of any particle cannons. Each Supership had assigned areas to attack. They flew in and started attacking their areas. Much of the population had left Washington DC after seeing the Superships earlier so the death toll should be low. From two miles above the surface the Superships did their jobs. However; the particle cannons could still detect the cloaked Superships.

The sensors that detected the Superships could not pinpoint the exact location of a cloaked ship but they got close. It took only fifteen minutes to totally destroy Washington DC but it cost Commander Kopi four of his Superships. His own ship was badly damaged but he managed to climb into space and out of range of the particle cannons.

Commander Kopi contacted Commodore Ail and reported that they had destroyed all of Washington DC except for the

White House. Then his communications was cut short when his ship blew up. With no one else around to help them those of the Kopi's crew that survived the attack and explosion died as the Supership burned in space. All one hundred fifty crewmen of the five Superships were killed in this attack.

When Commodore Ail contacted the King with his report Bubba just set back in his chair. He stared straight ahead and said nothing.

Knowing what happened Rommin asked his father; "You okay Dad?"

Bubba said nothing. His breathing was heavy. A part of him still loved Earth but he was tired of these Communist and Socialist Presidents and the people were responsible for electing them. "Kill'm all." he whispered but thank God no one heard him.

For over thirty minutes the King just sat in his chair staring straight ahead. Finally he told Rommin to leave him alone a few minutes. He needed to pray. When Rommin left the office and closed the door behind him Bubba bowed his head.

"Father ... I ... don't know ... what to do." Bubba said as he cried. *"I really need your guidance right now. Must I order the death of both of my children in order to end this?"*

Then Bubba got an idea. He went to the Comm Room and ordered Commodore Zu to send five thousand soldiers from Zim to Earth but hold fifty miles in space. Then he ordered Zu to send another two million soldiers to the same spot in space. There were not enough transport ships to do this so Zu had the transport ships drop of the soldiers in Northern Mexico and go back for more soldiers.

Stylus still had seventy-four Superships and sixty-five regular warships. With no known other threats all but ten warships were sent to Earth.

Not wanting to be a part of a Socialist government Texas had already been thinking of succeeding from the United States. Commander Ail took advantage of this and made a deal

140

with the Texas Governor. Commodore Zu had over two million soldiers which were moved into far northeast Texas where they held closer positions to Washington DC.

Once the citizens of Texas found out what was going on they even started helping the Stylus. It was exciting to work with soldiers from another planet. They had a common enemy with the Stylus; the dictator in Washington DC.

Finally Commander Ail sent regular warships with skeleton crews over the Texas border with Superships behind them. As they slowly worked their way towards Washington DC the particle cannons would fire on them. The Superships behind them would take out the particle cannons.

In some cases true American patriots took out some of the particle cannons. They never did like the Socialist President who turned dictator and did what they could to help the Stylus.

It took almost a full day but the warships and Superships finally worked their way to Washington DC. Only then did a Supership assigned to do this one thing swoop into Washington DC and over the White House. Instantly it transported Johm and Meshet to the ship and took off into space before it could be shot down. Only then did the remaining warships and Superships retreat into space.

This is when Commodore Zu had his soldiers transported into Washington DC where they unloaded off of the transport ships. Their first goal was to take over the White House. The second goal was to capture any citizens and American soldiers they found.

Johm was taken to the ship's Brig where the medical team revived him. Meshet was taken to a private room where she was also revived. No one knew that Meshet was really joining Johm because their father had ordered Johm's death so she kept it that way. There was no reason to let anyone know the truth. As far as anyone was concerned she just got mad at her father and went to get her brother before he was killed. At least that was what her report to the King was going to say.

While many of the Superships continued to destroy the particle cannons Commodore Ail had most of them return to

Stylus. Commander Pilk's Supership carried Johm and Meshet.

Just after leaving Earth Meshet went to the ship's Brig and talked with Johm. She admitted to him that she was going to join him but what had happened changed everything.

"I was going to join you to keep you safe but you're safe now." Meshet told her brother.

"What is the King going to do with me?" Johm asked.

"I don't know but he will not have you killed now." Meshet assured him. "The only reason he ordered your death was because you continued to cause the death of many Stylus."

"The Stylus are my enemy."

"You're stupid Johm." Meshet got angry. "That son of a whore that trained you brainwashed you. You saw the DNA report."

"I saw a doctored up report if that is what you mean." Johm insisted.

"Thinking like that will keep you in prison the rest of your life." Meshet said as she turned and left.

Johm thought about what Meshet said. She was right. Unless he wanted to spend the rest of his life in prison he had to pretend to go along with the idea that he was the King's son. He had to pretend that he believe the DNA test. He had to become a good actor.

Three days later the Superships arrived at Stylus Command. Commander Pilk landed his Supership at Stylus Command so that Johm could be taken directly to the palace. After landing Johm and Meshet were taken to a heavily guarded transport which took them to the palace. Meshet fallowed as Johm was taken under heavy guard to the palace jail. Once locked in a cell the security left leaving Meshet there looking at her brother.

At this time Johm started his acting. "How can I be sure that the DNA report is not doctored up?"

"You know it wasn't." Meshet insisted.

Johm had to appear to gradually change his way of thinking. Doing it suddenly would look so fake. He looked

142

down as if to look sad and Meshet fell for it. Then she saw his thoughts and knew that he was playing her as a fool.

"Damn you Johm." Meshet said. "You can't lie to me remember?"

Meshet stormed away leaving Johm to think. He knew that he had problems as long as Meshet was around.

"This is going to be harder than I thought." Johm whispered as he watched Meshet walk away. Then he started wondering if maybe she was telling him the truth. He did read the DNA report. What if it was not doctored up. What if he really was the King's son. He would be next in line to be King and his father was already very old. If he did this right he could do what ever he wanted as a future King of Stylus. He knew then that he had to convince himself that he really was the King's son and Meshet's twin brother.

Bubba did not want to see Johm until he calmed down some. As he tried to calm down Meshet was talking to him about Johm. With Johm actually trying to except what he was being told Meshet could see it in his thoughts. Then she relayed this to her father.

As Johm pretended to go along with what he was being told he actually started seeing that it was all true. As his brainwashing tried to fight back his memory also fought back. Then he started remembering how he thought before he started being taught by the Zim monk Stylum. He wondered if Stylum was even alive anymore. He had never heard that he was born a Zim until Stylum told him. He always knew that he was the King's son until Stylum started telling him different. Almost all of his thoughts started with the teachings of Stylum.

Armed with this new memory of when he started thinking that he was Zim he started realizing the truth. But he wondered how much of what he knew was a lie and what was the truth. He had to ask Meshet to help him which she happily did.

After four days Bubba went down to the palace jail and saw Johm. Part of him wanted to hug his son and part of him still wanted to have Johm executed.

143

"Hello Son." Bubba said from outside the cell.

Johm was laying on his bunk with his eyes closed but jumped up to see his the King. "Do I call you King or Father?" Johm said half way trying to put a guilt trip on Bubba.

"Which ever you want." Bubba replied.

"What do you plan to do with me?"

"Don't know yet." Bubba replied again. "You killed many Stylus not to mention the Zim that died because of the war you started." Almost one million have died because of you. Your life would not be worth a wet rock on Zim right now."

"I've heard that." Johm said.

"Why did you start that war and then leave them to fight it without you?" Bubba asked.

"Your soldiers were about to catch me so I left Zim."

"Well what happens to you is out of my hands now." Bubba said. "Many want you dead."

"And what do you want?" Johm asked.

Bubba thought for a moment. "I want my son back."

"I am back Dad."

"I want my son back not the murderer standing before me right now." Bubba said. "Do you happen to know where he is?" Bubba turned and left Johm standing there.

Chapter 14

Left Alone

Bubba knew that there was no way that he could just set Johm free. Over one million Stylus and Zim were now dead because of him. The day before Johm's trial he talked with Rommin and Meshet. He explained the spot that he was in and the citizens of Stylus would be watching what he did. And then there were those that he called Liberals because they were never happy no matter what he did.

Rommin and Meshet agreed with what their father said. They knew that if he freed Johm or even let him off easy the citizens of Stylus would come against him. He would be considered the worst King they ever had and he could not have that.

The next day Bubba sat in the chair behind the Judge's desk. Johm was brought in with six security walking him up to the front of the desk.

"Your name is Johm?" Bubba asked trying to keep it all professional.

"You know me Dad." Johm said with a smile.

Bubba took in a deep breath and let it out. "What I do today I do not want to do but … I must. The people of Stylus want justice and they expect their King to do the right thing."

"What are you doing Dad?" Johm asked. He thought that by starting to believe that he was the King's son that his father would be easy on him.

"I am doing my job to the best of my ability." he told Johm. You are charged with the deaths of over one million Stylus and Zim, treason against the Stylus government, and instigating a war against the people of stylus." Bubba looked at Johm who stood there with his mouth open. "How do you plea?"

"I … a …"Johm said not sure what else he should say. "… a … not guilty?"

Then Bubba allowed Johm to defend himself against all three charges. For the charge of killing over one million Stylus and Zim he said that they had their own choices and made bad decisions.

For the charge of treason he said that he just left Stylus to be a Holy Man but that did not come out until after his training from the Zim monk Stylum. Finally for the charge of instigating the war with Stylus on Zim he said that he tried to calm everyone down as their Holy Man. They went to war on their own.

"If you tried to stop them from rebelling then why do they blame you for their defeat?" Bubba asked.

"I don't know." Johm replied. He still did not believe that his father would give him much time.

"Johm. Stand boy." Bubba yelled. "I find you guilty on all three charges. I also sentence you to twenty years of hard labor in the Rock Quarry with no chance of parole. After you have served your twenty years you will be placed on probation where you will report to the Prime Minister twice a month."

Bubba sat in his chair silent. Johm could not say anything either. He did not believe that his father would give him such a long sentence.

"Your mad." Johm finally yelled. "Your crazy. Twenty years of hard labor?"

"Take him back to the palace jail." Bubba yelled. Then he turned to Johm and yelled; "I'll be seeing you before you're transported to your new home at the Rock Quarry."

Johm was drug out of the court room fighting the six security holding him. Most of them had lost loved ones because of the actions of Johm. On the way to the palace jail downstairs Johm fell a few times. By time he reached the jail he was in a lot of pain. Once he was locked up the security walked away laughing.

That night after Bubba finished his work he went straight upstairs to the bedroom. He and Becka talked about Johm until he fell asleep. For the past few days he had not been able to sleep because of his thinking about Johm. Now he could not stay awake.

Becka did as she had done a thousand times before. She rolled her husband over on his side and pulled out his arm in front of him. Then she lay beside him with the back of her shoulders against his chest. She lay her head on his arm and fell asleep. She knew that her King had to do what he did and backed his decision all the way. She cried for a while before falling asleep. She also loved her son.

Bubba did not sleep well that night. He tossed and turned all night. When Becka woke up at daybreak Bubba was already gone and in his office. Before long Meshet was in the office and getting back to the backlog of paperwork on her desk. When she walked into the office she sat at her desk and said nothing to her father.

"Are we speaking?" Bubba asked Meshet.

Meshet jumped. "Oh Dad." she said. "I didn't see you. You were so still and my mind was on … Johm."

"It's okay Meshet." Bubba said. With a smile. "He is upsetting us all right now."

"When are you having him transported to the Rock Quarry?" Meshet asked.

"I'll be going to see him later … if he will even talk to me." Bubba advised her.

"I can go with you and he might talk with you then." Meshet suggested.

Bubba thought about his daughter's offer and agreed. Then they both got busy with their work. Bubba read all of the reports that came across Meshet's desk and she had cleared for him.

In a report from Governor Coman on Zim the governor mentioned that everything was going well on the planet. The people had embraced his leadership although there were still a few that did not. He laughed when Coman called them his Liberals.

Later that day the King and Meshet went to the palace

jail. As they walked up to Johm's cell he started yelling. He was full of anger and rage. Bubba just stood there with a disappointed look on his face. He allowed his son to yell until he got tired.

"Are you finished acting like a spoiled child?" Bubba asked Johm. "Be a man for the first time in your life. You did this to yourself."

"Why are you doing this to me?" Johm asked yelling all the time.

"You did this to yourself." Bubba insisted again.

"Did you really expect that you would never be punished for what you did?" Meshet mentioned.

"I never thought that my father would give me twenty years in the Rock Quarry." Johm answered his sister. Then he looked at his father the King. "You hoping I will die in there?"

"Everyone on Stylus and Zim wanted you to be hung so that they could watch your death." Bubba informed his son. "No one has ever been hated so much."

"I don't give a damn." Johm yelled. "I hope you're still alive when I get out so I can hurt you like you're hurting me right now."

Bubba calmly turned and walked to the jailer. "Take him to the quarries when you want and then inform me when he is there."

"Yes Sir." the palace guard said.

As Johm continued to yell at his father Bubba walked away. Meshet stayed hoping to talk to her brother.

"What are you doing Johm?" Meshet asked.

Johm took in a deep breath and let it out trying to calm down. Sitting on the edge of his bed he held his face in his hands. He was trying to gain his sister's sympathy but she saw his thoughts and knew what he was trying.

"You're doing it again." Meshet said. As Johm looked up at her she continued. "You're faking it trying to get me on your side. Well let me tell you something. I was on your side but I see now that you will never change."

"You have never been on my side." Johm commented.

"Then why do you think I went to Earth." Meshet yelled. "Dad put out orders to have to killed on sight and I was hoping to save you."

With that last remark Meshet left the palace jail. Again Johm thought about what everyone had been telling him. Now he would be an old man by time he got out of the Rock Quarry. Looking down at the floor he prayed.

"Oh Muchee ... son of God, I have really messed up. Now I am about to spend the next twenty years busting up rocks with a hammer. Please help me ... out of this somehow."

Not even Johm knew that his disciples were planning to break him free. Joshen and four others had come to Stylus on a work order. Their real goal was to help Johm get free.

As the transport van pulled out of the palace gate and onto the street it turned towards the Rock Quarry. Just before getting to the quarry itself the van had to stop. A wheel had fallen off of a cart carrying rocks from the quarry. All four guards in the van got out. Two went to help the man get the wheel back on his cart while the other two stood guard outside the van. Suddenly the man with the cart pulled out a pistol and shot the two guards that came to help him. The other three disciples jumped out from behind walls and opened fire on the other two guards.

The four disciples jumped in the transport van and took off. Johm was free again. They quickly drove to a spot where a cargo ship was waiting. Quickly leaving the van and getting on board the cargo ship they took off before they could be stopped. By time the local police found the transport van the cargo ship was far off in space. By time Stylus Command found out what was going on the cargo ship was to far away to be tracked. No one knew where it went or even in which direction it went.

The King did not hear of Johm's escape for a few hours. Instantly the King put out an order that the cargo ship was to be destroyed on sight if found. Of course anyone finding a

149

cargo ship could not just fire at it because it may not be the one with Johm on board.

Just as Bubba and Meshet were leaving the palace to go home for the evening the King got a message from Commodore Ail. He had reported that a Supership under Commander Pilk found a cargo ship that had refused to stop for boarding. They did not fire on the cargo ship not knowing if it was the one with Johm on board.

The Supership that was chasing the cargo ship fired one warning shot across it's bow. The pilot of the cargo ship decided that running was not worth it and stopped. Three soldiers transported to the cargo ship. Minutes later they called back to their Commander. Johm was not on board and this was not the right cargo ship anyway.

"Sorry Sir." the Sergeant told his Commander. "All we have here is two young lovers that took the cargo ship without permission trying to get away from the girl's father."

"Who is the father?" the Commander asked.

"A ... Commodore Zu Sir."

"And they took the cargo ship without permission?"

"Yes Sir." the Sergeant replied.

"Put the two in our Brig and bring the cargo ship back to Stylus Command." the Commander ordered. "We will fallow you back to Stylus."

"Yes Commander." the Sergeant replied.

Back at the Palace Comm Room the King was listening to the conversations between the Commander and Sergeant. "He got away again." Bubba uttered.

"Father." Meshet said. "No matter how mad you are you cannot order the death of any Stylus citizen without a trial."

"But is Johm a Stylus citizen?" Bubba asked.

"You know he is Dad." Meshet insisted.

Bubba got back on the radio and called Commodore Ail. It took a few minutes but Ail finally got back to the King.

"Yes Sir." Ail said. "What can I do for you?"

"I am receding the order to kill Johm on sight." the King ordered. "He is to be captured ... if possible."

"And if he will not surrender?" Commodore Ail asked.

Bubba thought for a moment. He knew that Johm would only cause more trouble and even kill if he needed to. "If he cannot be captured then ... kill him and anyone with him."

"I can't believe you did it again." Meshet said. Like the last time her father ordered Johm's death she was standing behind him. He turned to look at her. "I don't have time for this Meshet."

"I brought him in last time." Meshet said. "Let me bring him in again."

"He won't come in again and you know it." Bubba told her. "Besides ... last time you did not really bring him in."

Meshet looked down. "I know Dad.

Bubba and Meshet went back to the King's office.

Johm knew that he could not go back to Zim because the people of Zim hated him so much. That left Noter 3, Sop 2, Mesh Ting 2, and a few other planets to run to and hide. After talking it over with his disciples he chose to go to Mesh Ting 2. No Stylus ships were patrolling it's airspace but just flying by every now and then. It had plenty of wild game to eat and water to drink. It also offered many caves in which they could live.

After dodging a few Stylus patrols the small cargo ship finally arrived at Mesh Ting 2 in four days. It took a few days but they did find a cave that was plenty big enough for the five of them. Now it was just a matter of moving the cargo that the disciples had loaded on the cargo ship before rescuing Johm.

Johm's attitude had changed a great deal. He now snapped at his disciples and hardly ever taught them the teachings of Muchee anymore. It did not take long before his disciples started staying away from him.

One morning Johm woke up and found the campfire had died during the night. Yelling about not having a fire to make his coffee Johm woke up the other four. Instead of making the fire like he had always done in the past he started throwing firewood at his disciples. When one of the chunks of wood hit Routen in the head he came flying up from his bedroll.

Yelling right in Johm's face Routen said; "The next time you hit me with anything I'll kick your ass."

Johm snickered. "Like you could do that."

That was all it took. Routen was walking away from Johm after yelling at him but quickly turned and hit Johm in the face knocking him down. Johm jumped back up and the fight was on. With all of the training hat Johm had in self defense he was having a hard time fighting Routen. Routen was a short hybrid and quicker than Johm who was a big hybrid. The two fought for a good fifteen minutes before quitting. They were both to tired to continue.

The other three disciples pulled Routen to one side leaving Johm to take care of himself. Backing up against the wall of the cave Johm looked at the four men that had been his friends. His anger towards them grew. For a long time Johm leaned back against the wall of the cave and just watched the other four. Finally he spoke.

"You four are the epitome of shame." Johm told his four disciples. "None of you are good disciples."

"None of us are your disciples anymore Johm." one of the men said. "You're to busy being an asshole."

Johm did not say anything else the rest of the night. He slept right there all night. The next morning he woke up and slowly climbed to his feet. He was more bruised up than he thought. Slowly he walked to the mouth of the cave and looked around. After a while he stepped outside the cave and walked around the area.

Finally Johm came to another cave that he liked. He did not want to be around the other four anymore. After building a fire at the mouth of the cave to mark it he went back to the others.

Johm asked the other four for one or two of the cases of food and a rifle for hunting. "Okay Johm." Routen said. "I'll give you a rifle for hunting but if you turn it on us we will kill you. Do you understand?"

"No problem." Johm agreed humbling himself.

Johm was still in a lot of pain so the disciples carried two of the ten cases of food to Johm's new home for him. Only there did Routen hand over a rifle to Johm.

"Remember Johm." Routen said. "If any of us accidentally get shot the rest of us will hunt you down and you will die. Otherwise we will leave you alone."

"And if I decide to go to another planet ... you have the cargo ship." Johm mentioned.

"Then we'll take you there." Routen said. But other than for that ... don't come around here again."

Johm nodded his head and turned. Walking away he knew that he was alone again. However; his survival training kicked in and he started using his training to survive.

Mesh Ting 2 was a heavily wooded planet with plenty of streams, rivers, and lakes. There was also plenty of animal life to hunt but Johm did not like harming an animal. When his survival training kicked in harming animals was put aside. Eating became more important.

Then one day Johm heard something outside. As he stepped out of the cave he saw the cargo ship fly overhead. He went to the cave where he other four had been staying. No one was there. Had they left him there? He did not know but he would not bother the things they left behind in case they came back. They had left some gear, ammo for the rifles, and four cases of food.

Johm left the cave and went back to his own cave. A week later he went back to the Disciple's cave and found that nothing had been bothered. They knew where his cave was but did not contact him before leaving. They had left him on Mesh Ting 2 alone.

The truth was that the four men had gone to Zim to try to buy more supplies. They had found a few precious stones in their cave but not many. They still had enough to buy some supplies. However; on their way to Zim they were spotted by a Stylus Supership and ordered to stop to be boarded. They chose to try to out run the Supership. Of course there was nothing that could out run a Supership; especially a cargo ship but, they tried.

153

The Supership fired a warning shot across the bow of the cargo ship but it did not even slow down. The next shot hit the port power cells causing the cargo ship to spiral down towards a planet that was to hot for any life forms. The Commander of the Supership tried to transport the crew of the Cargo ship on board but something in the atmosphere caused problems with their transporter. Finally the Supership got so close to the planet that they had to pull up or they would also crash into a molten lava lake. They barely made it but the cargo ship did not. It crashed into the molten lava lake and quickly sunk below the surface of the lava.

No one knew that Johm was on Mesh Ting 2. The Commander of the Supership that shot down the cargo ship reported that Johm was probably on board when it crashed into the molten lava of the planet.

At this time Johm was being haunted by all of the mistakes he had made in his life. So much of his life was wasted. He had thrown away any chance he had at living the way the son of a King should. Now he lived like an animal in a cave with no one to talk to.

Back on Stylus Meshet handed the report about the cargo ship being shot down to her father. When he read the part that mentioned that Johm was probably on board he started crying. Rommin and Meshet got on both sides of their father and held him. Then Becka and Tesh came into the office and asked why everyone was crying. Seconds later everyone was crying.

That evening Bubba sat at the desk in his and Becka's bedroom and looked at his computer. He tried to write what had happened to Johm but could not type. He managed to type a little but had to go back and make many corrections. When he went to bed Becka was already there. He lay beside her with his back to her. She lay her arm over her husband's waist. He slowly put his hand over her hand and pulled her arm tight around him. This was one of those times where he needed to be held.

Chapter 15

Galactic Peace

After not hearing from Johm in over a month Bubba and the family excepted that he had died when the cargo ship crashed into the molten lave lake. The planet's name was Hell 13. Meshet had not seen any of Johm's thoughts during this time so he had to have been dead.

No one knew it but Mesh Ting 2 had an atmosphere that actually blocked the mental telepathy between Johm and Meshet. Many times Johm and Meshet tried to contact each other but with no results. As far as Bubba and his family knew Johm was dead.

While the family prepared for the funeral for Johm, Johm himself was striving to survive alone on Mesh Ting 2. He soon ran out of ammunition for the rifle and had to depend on building and setting traps. He also found a few plants that tasted good and grew them in a garden. He found a few fruit trees and dug up the smaller ones. Transplanting them closer to the cave they did well.

Although the family had a funeral for Johm the citizens of Stylus and Zim celebrated his death. The citizens were happy to hear about Johm's death. Celebrations lasting through the week popped up everyplace.

A coffin was made and many of Johm's things were placed in it. Then in a private ceremony the coffin was buried on the palace grounds behind the palace to keep anyone from destroying the headstone or the grave.

For almost a week the citizens of Stylus celebrated Johm's death but Bubba did nothing about it. He understood how they felt. The Royal Family did not do much work that week but just took care of the things that had to be taken care of. All of the women spent the week crying while the men saw to their needs.

Bubba called off the patrols that were looking for Johm. This meant that Mesh Ting 2 was no longer patrolled and all hopes of Johm being rescued was lost. Of course Johm did not know this.

On Mesh Ting 2 Johm was doing well surviving off of the land. He noticed what the monkeys were eating and tried it for himself. As for meat the monkeys were the easiest to catch in traps.

One day Johm was out checking his traps when a large animal that looked much like a grizzly bear came upon Johm. Armed only with a long pole that he had sharpened to a point at one end Johm turned to fight the bear.

The bear stood on it's back legs and slowly walked towards Johm. Johm turned again and ran but with the bear running on all four legs quickly caught up with Johm. When Johm stopped to fight the bear stood on it's back legs again. Johm saw that he would have to make his fight right there. On all four legs the bear would only out run him.

When the bear walked close enough Johm lunged forward and stabbed it in the chest piercing the bear's heart. The bear came down breaking Johm's spear leaving him with no weapon at all. However; an animal has not knowledge of death so the bear came after Johm again. The struggle did not last long because the bear's heart had stopped with a sharp pole through it. By time the bear fell over Johm had received many cuts from the bear's long claws.

Tearing his clothes into strips he tied them over the cuts to stop the bleeding. Then he slowly walked back to his cave where he had more bandages from the cases left by the four disciples. One of the cases was full of medical supplies.

Johm managed to stop the bleeding but he was messed up. He fed the fire and set back against a rock and rested. He was weak and the medical supplies had no anti-biotics.

"Muchee ... son of God ... I am hurt bad. That bear really tore me up some and I was not even able to carry any meat back.

156

I need that meat to help heal me. I need ... my father. I need to get back ..."

Johm passed out in the middle of his prayer. He was weak and still bleeding some. Without help and anti-biotics he stood no chance. Johm slipped into adeep sleep. He would never wake up again.

Governor Coman was having a time with the Liberals on Zim. Most of the citizens were happy. Unemployment was very low and there were plenty of empty jobs for anyone looking for work. Working with his father he and the King of Stylus worked out a plan to transport workers to where ever they were needed.

Prompt 4 had many mines of all types that needed workers willing to go into a mine and work. That kind of work was not for everyone. Prompt 4 also had many ranches that raised Bocka, a large animal that looked much like cattle on Earth. However; the Bocka were larger.

Most of Prompt 4 was a desert. These deserts were cool at night and had the Ouvo frogs that came out at night. No one knew how the Ouvo frogs were on Stylus, Zim, and Prompt 4 but they were.

Prompt 4 also had a few rivers and lakes but not many. In these areas farmers grew what they could. Before long food was plentiful and being shipped out to other planets that needed it.

Workers were being sent back to Noter 3 to continue scrapping the crashed ships from so long ago. This not only brought in workers but all of the supplies that they needed.

Back on Stylus Bubba was starting to get back to work. The celebrations over Johm's death had already stopped and the citizens were back to doing what they normally did.

The Milky Way Galaxy was finally under control. Stylus pretty much ran everything except for Earth. Earth remained a problem. President Marks of the United States as well as Russia and China were still a problem. Other countries on Earth might also pose a problem.

Bubba called in his war staff for a meeting. It included Commodore Zu, Commodore Ail, Prime Minster Rommin and a few others. In this meeting he worked out a plan to go to Earth and talk to the leaders of different countries. Earth would come under the rule of Stylus or be destroyed. They would not be a threat to the galaxy again.

It was decided that the Prime Minister would go to Earth and not the King. Bubba was an old man now and would not be able to do the job. Commander Pilk now commanded ten Superships that patrolled Earth's airspace. He had only commanded five Superships but with this new plan to contact earth he was given five more.

It took Rommin four days to get to Earth but he took another squadron of Superships with him in case they were needed. This Squadron was Commander by Commander Revis, Bubba's son-in-law. He was married to Bubba's daughter Lesst.

Once Rommin got to Earth he contacted President Marks of the United States.

"Don't come around here or I'll destroy all of your ships." Marks said.

"Yeah ... like you did last time right?" Rommin said as he laughed. "Listen up."

"No!" Marks insisted. "You listen up."

Rommin turned to Commander Revis and said; "Fire on the White House ... it's west wing." Rommin ordered. He also said it over the microphone so that Marks could hear the order.

Seconds later the West Wing of the White House was leveled; again.

"Now like I said ... Listen up." Rommin told Marks. "Or should I level the East Wing as well?"

"There's no need for that." Marks gave in. "What do you need?"

"I need you to contact the leaders of other countries and set up a meeting for one week from now. At this meeting I will discuss with them the terms for their surrender."

"Are you crazy." Marks yelled. "You actually want the

entire planet to surrender to you?"

"Well ... it is not as bad as you think." Rommin said. "You would be allowed to continue running your own countries but the fighting among yourselves would stop."

"They won't go for that." Marks argued.

"Anyone that does not go for that will be destroyed." Rommin reminded Marks. "Now set up the meeting. I will send security down to see to the security of the meeting place. If anyone harms any of the security I send down I will destroy that country without any warning."

"I'll try." Marks said. Then he heard the click of Rommin's microphone and he knew that the communications were over. He set back in his chair and thought for a moment. Then he got busy contacting the leaders of the most powerful countries.

Four days later Marks called for Rommin and said that the meeting would take place in the United Nations Building in New York City. Rommin agreed and insisted that the entire building be emptied as quickly as possible. Then he would send Stylus soldier to make sure that the building was cleared.

"I'll take care of the security there." Marks ordered loudly.

"Mister President." Rommin calmly said. "Just how much do you like that East Wing?"

"Oh ... okay." Marks gave in again. He was not used to this.

"Thank you Sir." Rommin said trying to show some respect. "Let me know when the building is empty and then I will send my soldiers."

"Will do." Marks agreed.

Early the next morning Marks contacted Rommin and told him that the building was empty. Rommin sent one hundred well armed soldiers from a transport ship that Commander Revis brought with him.

The Stylus solders walked through the building and cleared it for Rommin. Rommin did this for his own safety. He did not want the American President to set up someone to shoot him.

On the day of the meeting the Stylus soldiers filled the walkways to the United Nations Building. Seven stood outside the main door with another ten just inside. There was no doubt as to who was in charge. Just to make sure that everyone knew not to mess with Prime Minister Rommin he had four Superships hover just above the buildings on all four sides of the United Nations Building.

When all of the world leaders were at their places Rommin transported behind the podium. The four Superships engaged their shields and uncloaked so that everyone could see them.

The room full of the well armed Stylus soldiers. It got quiet when Rommin suddenly appeared. Everyone looked at the Stylus hybrid who for a while just looked around. Then finally Rommin spoke.

"I am Prime Minister Rommin of the planet Stylus. I am here today to offer you peace. If you except it then you will have trade with other planets in this galaxy. If you do not except my offer then you will be destroyed and others will be given your land. It is that simple."

"Who are you to come here and order us to surrender our countries to you?" China asked.

"Our galaxy has been in turmoil for many years. This turmoil has ended with Earth being the only planet in the galaxy still fighting. This fighting will stop as of now."

"But we have enemies." the leader of Iran said. What should we do? The Qur'an tells us to kill all nonbelievers."

"I have read your Qur'an and ... although it says over and over that Allah is all merciful it tells you to kill. Where is the mercy? However; you may still worship any way you wish but the killing of Christians or anyone else that does not believe like you do will stop."

Rommin went on for three hours answering question from the leaders of Earth. Finally he stopped and transported back to his ship. The leaders of Earth were left to decide on what they would do. China and Russia did not like giving up total control of their countries while other countries that were afraid of China's and Russia's aggression liked what Rommin offered. Marks was tired of rebuilding his White House and also finally agreed.

Rommin was tired. The whole time he was standing there he was afraid that someone would try to shoot him. He went to his room and had dinner brought to him. A large plate holding a Bocka steak was set in front of him.

"Medium rare." the cook said. "Just like you like it Prime Minister."

"Thank you very much." Rommin told the cook. As the cook left Rommin prayed over the meal and then dug in with his sharp knife and fork. After eating he walked up to the Bridge and talked with Commander Revis for a while. Then he went back to his room and to bed. He had, had a long day.

The next morning Rommin contacted Marks to see how the leaders of Earth voted. Only Russia and China voted against Rommin's offer. With all of the leaders still in New York Rommin called for another meeting that evening. All of the leaders were told of the meeting and were at their places in the United Nations Building.

As the day before, it got quiet when Rommin transported into the room and behind the podium. Again Rommin looked over the crowd as it got quiet. Only then did he speak.

"I hear that everyone wants to except my offer except for Russia and China. Is this true?" Rommin asked as he looked right at the leader of the two countries. "May I ask why?"

"My family has run China for many years. I do not want that to change."

"But that would not change." Rommin assured the leader of China. The fighting among your countries must stop though. You must also get rid of any weapons of mass destruction. In return we will see that you have trade with other planets. This will only profit you."

"And what will keep other countries from attacking us?" the leader of Russia asked.

"We will." Rommin said. "Any aggression from one country on another will answer to us. Earth is the only planet in this galaxy where the people fight among themselves. It's time to start living in harmony with each other."

"And what if we do not want to live in this harmony with neighboring countries?" Iran asked.

"Then we will simply destroy you." Rommin said. "It is simple. You will except this offer or your countries will be destroyed."

The leaders of Russia and China talked for a while and then agreed to the peace that Rommin offered. Earth was finally going to see total peace. They also agreed to be policed to make sure that all rules were obeyed. All life in the Milky Way Galaxy was finally at peace.

Bubba; now King of the galaxy died one year after this peace with Earth. Missing him very much Becka died a month later. Many said that she could not live without her husband by her side. Sleeping at night was almost impossible without laying on his arm.

Bubba's birthday became a holiday that was celebrated on every planet in the galaxy. Bubba had come from being just another man on Earth to ruler of the Milky Way Galaxy. No one had ever come so far.

Rommin became the King of not only Stylus but the entire galaxy. He and Tesh had two sons that were raised to be proud Stylus citizens and perfect leaders for the future.

The prophecy of the Prophecy Twins never came to pass. Bubba was the one that stopped the fight between the planets Zim and Stylus. Johm had a lot to do with the fighting and Meshet had a lot to do with the end of the fighting but as twins they ended nothing together.

Many years later someone found human bones in a cave on Mesh Ting 2. The bones were brought back and DNA was taken from them. This was after the death of King Bubba and Becka so they died never really knowing what happened to their son. King Rommin had Johm's coffin dug up and his bones places in it. Then Johm was finally properly buried. At least the rest of the family found him.

The legend of Bubba, the man from Earth became a story

that every child in the galaxy was taught. There was no one in the Galaxy that did not know who King Bubba was. He was a King known simply by his nickname; Bubba.

Other Publications of

Vernon Gillen

Below is a list of my other novels and books that have been published.

Published Novels

1. "Texas Under Siege 1."
   Tale of a Survival Group Leader.
   After a man is voted as the leader of his survival group in Texas a self proclaimed Marxist president asked the United Nations troops to come in and settle down the civil unrest. The civil unrest was really nothing but Americans that complained about how he ran the country.

2. "Texas Under Siege 2."
   The Coming Storms.
   The young group leader continues to fight when the countries that made up the United Nations troops in the United States decided to take over parts of the country for their own country's to control.

3. "Texas Under Siege 3."
   The Necro Mortises Virus.
   As the group leader continues to fight the UN he learns that an old organization really controlled everything. They were known as the Bilderbergs. Tired of the resistance in Texas they release the Necro Mortises virus also known as the zombie virus.

4. "Texas Under Siege 4."
   250 Years Later.

This novel jumps 250 years into the future where the Bilderbergs are still living with modern technology while the other people have been reduced to living like the American Indians of the early 1800's. One of these young man stands up and fights the Bilderbergs with simple spears and arrows.

5. The Mountain Ghost 2."
   The Legend Continues.
   The Mountain Ghost continues to fight the Chinese and North Koreans soldiers that have invaded the entire southern half of the United States.

6. "The Mountain Ghost 4."
   The Ghost Warriors.
   After Russ and June have twin girls they grow up and move back south to fight the Chinese and North Koreans as the Ghost Twins. Before long they grow in numbers and call themselves the Ghost Warriors.

7. "Neanderthal 1."
   As a child he was injected with alien DNA. While in the Navy he was injected with Neanderthal DNA. Now because of these two injection without his knowing young Michael Gibbins changes into a six and a half foot tall Neanderthal from time to time. He grew up being bullied in school and wished that he could change into a monster so he could get back at them. Now he wishes he could take that wish back.

8. " Neanderthal 2."
   Little Mary Ann, the daughter of Michael and Evie grows to the age of thirteen. As she grows she learns that he has many of the same abilities that her father had; and more. The problem is that she has a hard time controlling them and her anger. This causes problems for everyone watching over and trying to hide her.

9. "My Alien Connections 1."

After learning that he has been abducted many times over the years sixty-four year old Bubba is asked to be a part in an alien experiment. He ends up falling in love with an alien hybrid that has known through all of his abductions.

But the Aliens, the Stylus are at war with another planet, the Zims. As their war continues the Zim try to take the twins born to Bubba and his alien hybrid wife who have been prophesied hundreds of years earlier. Do the Zim win or does Bubba win?

10. "My Alien Connection 2"

After the American President turns against Bubba he and Becka move to the planet Stylus. After a while the American President breaks his agreement with Yunnan, the leader of the Stylus world and Bubba goes on the attack. When the American President becomes an ally with the Zim home world the war between Stylus and Zim thickens.

Through all of this Bubba and Becka must fight the Zim that are constantly trying to kidnap their twins which are the Prophecy Twins of Stylus. Fighting this war on many fronts Bubba is given control of Stylus warships and brings the fighting to the planet Zim.

11. "My Alien Connection 3"

As the Prophecy Twins grow up they learn many things and go through a few hardships. But they had always had each other until there is a betrayal in the family. Someone in the family turns to help the enemy causing problems for all Stylus.

How will Bubba and Becka handle this? How will the citizens of Stylus handle this? What will the twins do about this? Who even is the traitor?

Other Published Books

1. "Carnivores of Modern Day Texas."

A study of the animals in Texas that will not only kill you

but in most cases will eat you.

2. "Zombies; According to Bubba"
   After studying the Necro Mortises virus for my novel *Texas Under Siege 3*, I realized that I had a great deal of information on it. After finishing the novel I wrote this book leaving the reader to make their own decision.

Unpublished

A great deal goes into publishing a novel or book that takes time. After I write a novel I have someone proofread it. Then I have to find an artist to draw the cover picture which is hard to do. Actually finding an artist is easy but finding one that I can afford is not so easy. Then the novel or book has to be approved by the publishing company. Only then is it published. Then you have kindle and that opens another can of worms.

The fallowing novels are unpublished as I write this but will be published soon. Keep checking Amazom.com for any new novels that I have published.

1. "The Mountain Ghost 1."
   The Legend of Russell Blake.
   After the Chinese and North Koreans attack the southern United States two young brothers, Brandon and Russell Blake go after the invading enemy. After Brandon is killed Russell smears a white past allover his exposed skin and earns the name Mountain Ghost.

3. "The Mountain Ghost 3."
   The Ghost Soldiers.
   After the death of Russell Black his son, Russ, continues as to bring death and destruction to the enemy as the new Mountain Ghost.

5. "The Glassy War."
   Three thousand years in the future and three galaxies

away the United Planet Counsel fight and enemy that is trying to control every galaxy they come to. After both star ships crash into the planet the survivors continue to fight.

6. "The Fire Dancers."
I stopped writing this novel to start writing the Mountain Ghost series but I will be getting back to it.

I hope that you have enjoyed this novel. Please help me by sending your comments on what you thought about this novel or book by contact me through my web site at http://cabubba7.wexsite.com/bubbasbooks . By doing this you will let me know what you, the public, are looking for in these types of novels and books. I have a very creative mind, a bit warped some say but, still creative but, I still need to know what you are looking for. I thank you for your assistance in this.

Vernon Gillen

Made in the USA
Columbia, SC
16 November 2022

71175829R00093